The Reluctant Santa

By Sylvia McDaniel

Books by Sylvia McDaniel

Contemporary Romance

Standalones
The Reluctant Santa
My Sister's Boyfriend
The Wanted Bride
The Relationship Coach
Her Christmas Lie
Secrets, Lies, and Online Dating
Paying for the Past
Cupid's Revenge

Anthologies
Kisses, Laughter & Love
Christmas with you

Collaborative Series

Magic, New Mexico
Touch of Decadence

Western Historicals

Standalones
A Hero's Heart
A Scarlet Bride
Second Chance Cowboy

The Cuvier Women
Wronged
Betrayed
Beguiled

Lipstick and Lead
Desperate
Deadly
Dangerous
Daring
Determined
Deceived

Scandalous Suffragettes
Abigail
Bella
Callie
Faith

The Burnett Brides
The Rancher Takes a Bride
The Outlaw Takes a Bride
The Marshal Takes a Bride
The Christmas Bride

Anthologies
Wild Western Women
Courting the West
Wild Western Women Ride Again

Collaborative Series

The Surprise Brides
Ethan

American Mail Order Brides
Katie

The Reluctant Santa
Published by Virtual Bookseller

Cover Design by Kim Killion
http://thekilliongroupinc.com/

Edited by Andrea Dickinson
http://www.qualitybookservices.com/

Formatted by Laurelle Procter
laurelleprocter@gmail.com

Short Description: This year, two angels are giving Colin McDermott everything he didn't want. A Santa suit, a child, and a chance at love again.

ISBN: 978-1-942608-44-8 (paperback)
ISBN: 978-1-942608-45-5 (e-book)

{Contemporary Romance – Fiction}
{Holiday Romance – Fiction}

www.SylviaMcDaniel.com

Synopsis

Since his mother abandoned him on Christmas Eve never to return, Colin McDermott has hated Christmas and sworn never to have children. But this year two angels are giving him everything he didn't want. A Santa suit, a child, and a chance at love again. This is his last chance to learn the true meaning of Christmas.

Table of Contents

Chapter One

"His soul is mine," Devon, the devil's angel, said. He watched the humans, who were oblivious to his presence, gathered in the sales office. One of the best things about being an angel was his ability to pop into just about anywhere and spy on his subjects without their knowledge. He could observe the humans as if were watching a play and even occasionally act as director.

A chill wind howled outside the downtown Denver office, heralding the arrival of winter and the holiday season, the perfect time of year to increase his soul count. Devon studied his next soul, a brown-haired young man with expressive brows and a quirky grin. Unbeknownst to him, the salesman's life meter was about to expire unless he made drastic changes.

"Devon," a voice echoed into the atmosphere before the being that irritated him the most shimmered into his vision. "Doing a soul count before he's yours?"

Slowly, an angel materialized, clad from head to toe in a white leather jacket and white knee-high boots fit snug over white leather pants. A gold belt around her waist, held a cross that signified sergeant, angel, first class. Her halo was tilted at a rakish angle. In earth terms, Gabriella looked hot.

"Whoever is in charge of your wardrobe, I like the changes they've made," Devon said, letting his eyes rake her until a searing heat reminded him he was crossing boundaries. "Please tell me they ditched the boring robes."

With a toss of her blonde hair, her blue eyes flashed, glinting silver as her brows rose.

"My robes are hardly boring, but no, one of my cases is a motorcyclist. I'm riding shotgun today, trying to keep him from splattering all over the highway. The robes kept blowing up in my face, so I found a solution."

"Nice!" Devon shook his head and forced his eyes back to the human whose life he'd soon influence. "I thought your promotion at Easter took you out of the saving souls division."

Gabriella smiled as the air around her shimmered. Why didn't the angels from purgatory patrol get that shimmery essence?

"Devon, we work so…well together" she said, drawing out the word until he wanted to snap at her. He held onto his temper.

"We're all looking for ways to make quota this time of year. Only the strongest stay out of the pit, and every time I come up against you, I lose. But not this time. This one belongs to me," he announced, staring at the man whose only interest in life was making money. No family, no girlfriends, no friends— just work and money.

Gabriella tsked. "Now why would you want to send this poor man to hell for eternity? He just needs a little coaxing to choose the right path."

Devon sighed. "His time is about to expire. I'm here to collect his soul."

"Maybe," she said. "Unless, I can give him some guidance and save him from evil."

"Not this time. Heavenly angels may not be able to play dirty, but I can," he said, smiling at Gabriella. "And I intend to win this one."
Gabriella laughed.

"Always so arrogant, Devon." She glanced at their human. "His case is challenging, but I'm certain I can help him."

She turned toward Devon, her brows rising. "Playing dirty landed you where you are now. Why should I expect anything less?"

"How I got here doesn't matter. I need this soul," he snapped. "You make your soul count or the big man sends you back to the pit to fight and claw your way back for another chance."

"And Colin McDermott needs to be saved," Gabriella said, swirling back to their subject. "I mean, look at the poor man. He has no idea his priorities are in the wrong place. He's a selfish, greedy man because he's unloved."

"Love!" Devon exclaimed. "You heavenly angels think loving someone solves everything."

Gabriella shook her head at Devon, her blue eyes darkening with some sort of power. "Even you deserved love, Devon. In fact, if I had been your angel, I would found someone to show you love. Hopefully, you'd have been smart enough to grab the lifeline."

"Well, you weren't my angel, and now I'm the big man's soul catcher."

"It's simple, Devon. Why would you want to lure more men into the darkness you already face?" she asked.

Devon clenched his fist, struggling to control the frustration that spiraled through him. Hell was not a place anyone planned on going. "The pit!" he said. "Let's just concentrate on the human."

"I already was." She contemplated Colin McDermott. "He's quite handsome with those long, sandy lashes and sparkling honey eyes. If I were human, one look and he'd melt my heart."

"Women on earth know he's not a good risk. I could wrap this case up before Christmas, if you weren't here."

"Too bad. I'm here to keep you from destroying him," she said, giving him a stern frown. "The poor soul has no idea of what he's about to face. I'm sure you've got some nasty surprises in store for him, some hard to resist temptations. But hopefully, with my guidance, he'll make the changes his life needs."

Devon shook his head. "No, by Christmas he'll be mine. Count on it."

~

Colin McDermott sat across from his boss in the Denver headquarters of ECM Rx Software Incorporated. Dressed in his best suit and tie, trying not to fidget, he waited for his boss to announce the new western director of sales.

For the last six months, Colin had maintained the highest sales of any of the producers in his district. Logan Spencer had been his closest competitor, but Colin knew Logan had failed to beat him.

With four short weeks until the start of the new year, the sales director's position in the California office must be filled before December 26. The new director had to pull the sales team together and calculate the projections for the next year. In the next three weeks, he had to be on the ground and working that division.

Colin had the highest sales numbers in the company. The position was his.

"As you know the reason I called the two of you to my office is about the sales director's position. All year Colin's been number one with Logan trailing close behind at number two. Unfortunately, I can only name one of you western sales director, and your year-to-date sales are now dead even."

Colin glanced over at Logan, and the man grinned at him. The bastard had to have sold something substantial in the last week to have tied him. For months Colin had sacrificed his personal life, worked nights, six and seven days a week, yet Logan had managed to catch him.

Colin glanced at Ed Tieger, his mentor, the man who'd taught him everything he knew about sales. He refused to meet his gaze directly.

"I've spoken to the president of the company. We've decided to make this a competition." The older man folded his hands on top of his desk and leaned toward the two of them. "To help boost our year-end sales figures and to find out which of you has the most drive to acquire this position, we're issuing a challenge. Whoever brings in the highest sales numbers in the next three weeks will be the new western sales director. This competition involves no one else on the sales force. Just the two of you."

"But I had the most sales," Colin objected, acutely aware of how hard he'd worked in the last six months to win this position.

Ed nodded, his gaze steadfast on Logan. "But now less than a hundred dollars separates the two of you."

He gave each man a hard, long look that caused Colin's gut to clench with dread. "Three weeks, gentleman. May the best salesman win."

Colin stood and shook Logan's hand while he leaned in close. "Best of luck to you, but that position is mine."

Logan laughed. "I snuck up on you last month. I can do it again." He released Colin's hand and slapped him on the back. "Don't slow down long enough to look over your shoulder, or I'll blow right on by you."

A surge of determination roared through Colin.

Game on. The position belonged to him.

He walked out of the office, taking the stairs two at a time, ready to tackle the task and prove once and for all that Colin McDermott was the best man for the job.

Pushing open the glass door leading outside the office building, he stepped into the frigid air and drew his coat closer as the wave of cold hit him.

The repetitive ringing of a bell drew his attention to a man dressed as Santa. A red kettle stood beside the entrance to the office. The man's smile drew his attention to the kettle, and the memory of a frightened little boy sleeping inside a Salvation Army homeless shelter reminded him of where he'd come from. He never wanted to be homeless again.

That promotion would be his.

He looked at the man closely, "George is that you?"

The older man laughed. "Hey, how are you, Colin? Are you working the food line for us this Saturday?"

Colin shook his head, "No, something has come up. I'll be working here." He tilted his head toward the building.

"That's a shame. The guys enjoy it when you serve. They'll miss you."

"Tell the men I hope to be back next weekend. I'll definitely be in before Christmas."

Colin yanked out his wallet, pulled out a hundred, and stuffed it into the kettle.

"Thanks, Colin. Merry Christmas."

"Merry Christmas, George." Colin hated Christmas, but hell, it could have been the Fourth of July and he would have donated. He knew how much the shelter needed the cash. His donation wasn't about Christmas, it was about surviving another day.

~

Brooke Warren watched as her best friend and coworker Amelia Carter stepped onto the elevator.

"We have no Santa," Amelia Carter said, raising her hands dramatically as the elevator slid toward the hospital's administrative floor. "And the party is in less than an hour."

"What happened?" Brooke asked, thankful they were alone.

Amelia rolled her blue eyes. "While putting on his Santa costume, the old geezer fell in the men's room and hit his head on the floor. The janitor found him passed out cold. Seems he'd been celebrating the holiday season a little early. His blood alcohol level was two point zero."

"Oh my God!" Brooke said, horrified at the thought that the children in the hospital had almost been exposed to a drunken Santa Claus. As assistant administrator, her mind immediately went to the publicity nightmare this could have caused. *News at ten, drunken hospital Santa listens to sick children's wishes.*

"Is he all right?" she asked, concerned for the poor man and not wanting the hospital involved in a lawsuit.

"Yeah, first we bandaged his bleeding head and then security called the cops, who cuffed Santa and took him to jail for public intoxication. He'll be detoxing in a cell for several days."

"What are you going to do? The children are expecting Santa this afternoon."

"I don't know. My secretary is on the phone right now, trying to find any available Santa before the party," Amelia said, tossing her long blonde hair.

With a personality that attracted children, Amelia was perfect as the person in charge of charity work at the hospital. People gravitated toward her, and she raised a lot of donations for the small hospital.

Brooke shook her head, distressed at the idea of the children not seeing Santa. "You have a party scheduled on every floor for the next three weeks. It's a little late in the season to start searching for a new Santa."

How could she help her friend? Brooke liked to think that while they healed people, she made certain their hospital had the best work and patient environment possible.

"So far, I can't even find a suit."

"Wow," Brooke said. "That really sucks."

They reached the office door, and Amelia halted. "Gotta run see if Joyce has located either a suit or a Santa."

"Yeah, I've got a meeting in five minutes with a pharmaceutical rep. If you find a suit, I'll be Santa," Brooke volunteered. "But just for today."

Amelia laughed. "God, I love you. I may have no

choice but to take you up on your offer. I would do it, but I'm in charge of making certain that every child gets something from the hospital besides a whiff of Santa's alcoholic breath."

"We can't disappoint the children," Brooke said. "I know. If I find a suit, you're on."

"Talk to you later," Amelia said, hurrying off toward her office.

Brooke turned toward the conference room, wondering how quickly she could end this meeting. She opened the door, surprised to see the hospital's IT director there ahead of her. She hadn't known he planned to attend.

The small room held a large table and chairs centered in the middle with a beverage area in the back. Bob, the IT director, turned and moved toward her, his tall, lanky frame blocking her view of the drug sales rep. "Brooke, there's someone here I'd like you to meet. He's working for a company that could possibly save us thousands in drug costs."

He moved to the side and Brooke felt her mouth fall to the floor.

Oh Damn! Oh Damn! Oh my God, she hadn't seen that face in years.

There in front of her stood her college sweetheart, the man she'd thought she would marry. The man she'd fallen in love with and dreamed of spending the rest of her life with until that fateful day when he'd rejected her, and unknowingly, the baby she'd carried.

Tall, strikingly handsome, muscular, with a boyish grin and sparkling honey-warm eyes, Colin McDermott grinned at her like she was lunch and he was starving.

~

Colin stared in disbelief at Brooke Warren, the girl who'd dumped him in college. Right before graduation, she'd abruptly stopped seeing him, refused his telephone calls and disappeared from campus. Later, he'd learned she had finished her exams and hadn't waited on graduation but immediately left town, leaving him bitter and disillusioned.

Shocked, he studied her as the memory of that time seemed to rise from the shadows. Didn't he deserve an explanation? A reason why she'd ended their relationship so abruptly that she couldn't even say good-bye?

Memories of the way her gorgeous red hair had fallen across his shoulders when he'd made love to her flashed through his mind and left him aching.

Yeah, he'd do her again given half the chance. This time, he'd just disengage his heart. Because she'd left his fragile organ bloodied, bruised, and sporting a no admittance sign.

Emerald eyes focused on him in surprise as she held out her hand. All the anger at her disappearance threatened to surface and choke him, but he pushed it down deep. He needed this sale, even if it meant kissing up to the girl who'd lied and said she loved him one moment and played Houdini the next.

"Er…nice to see you again, Colin," she said, grasping his hand, her body stiff. Quickly she stepped back.

Her touch was warm, her hand soft, as he looked into eyes that reminded him of emerald Irish hills and ignited a spark in his midsection.

Damn, she was even better looking than she had been in college. Where once were sharp angles, now soft, round curves lay beneath her clothes. Her auburn hair called to mind russet sunsets in spring and awakened a pang of memories—the two of them studying together, the way she looked while she slept, and the night of his frat party when they'd both consumed the spiked punch and had wild monkey sex.

Young and naïve, he'd thought they'd always be together, but she'd run out just like everyone he'd ever cared about. She'd disappeared from campus, and he'd never seen her again until today.

Since that lesson, his focus remained on making his first million and never looking back. And this new position would get him one step closer to his dream.

"Since you guys know each other, I'm going to leave you," the IT director said. "Colin, call me if I can answer any of your questions."

"Thanks, Bob," Colin replied, as Bob walked out the door, leaving them alone. She was probably married with a couple of kids by now. Yet he yearned to ask her why she'd vanished leaving him to wonder what he'd done wrong.

Inhaling a deep breath, determined to concentrate on now and not the past, he unfurled his clenched fists. He needed this sale, so how could he ease the tension in the room and get the appointment?

"Wow, you look great. As beautiful as right before we graduated," he said, hoping that tense little smile on her face would soften. If she was the gatekeeper, he was in deep trouble. A sale to her hospital was necessary to his success.

"Thank you," she said, staring at him, hardly moving.

She wasn't falling all over herself after not having seen him for six years. He pictured a big red stop sign on Brooke's beautiful, flawless face. She wanted no part of him. His first priority would be getting past her to the decision makers.

"How have you been?" he asked, wondering how she'd wound up here in this small town hospital and wishing he could ask her what he *really* wanted to know.

"Wonderful," she replied, not asking about him. She glanced down at her watch. "Look, I need to make this quick."

So much for a happy reunion. She wanted him gone, and quickly.

"Yeah, I know my time with you today was for only thirty minutes, but I wanted to give you an overview of how our product could help Crystal Mountain's number one hospital."

They were all number one hospitals, but she didn't need to know that.

"Colin, our pharmaceutical contract is not up for bidding at this time. Leave me your card and phone number, and I'll be sure to contact you before our contract renews." She started to walk away.

He gave a little chuckle. Stop sign number one. "I'm not a pharmaceutical rep. Our product helps hospitals track their drug purchases and how much they're spending and makes certain you're not being overcharged for the medications on your contract."

She gave him a look that said he could be selling gold bricks at half price and she'd still show him the door, and probably slam and lock it behind him.

Her lips turned up in a smile that didn't quit reach her eyes. "Your product may help reduce costs, but right now is not the time for me to consider a purchase like this for our hospital. I'll call you when we're interested."

"On January 1 the price goes up over five thousand dollars," he said, not totally dishonest, just slightly exaggerating the truth. "Bob put us in touch with you," he reminded her. "He thought the hospital could save a lot of money using our product."

"Give me your card and I'll contact you after the first of the year."

The door burst open as a blonde-haired woman ran into the conference room out of breath and panting. "Sorry, but I can't wait. I've got a suit. The party is in fifteen minutes."

Colin watched the two women's eyes communicate

without saying a word. Slowly they turned and observed him, and an uneasy feeling settled around him at the tension in the room.

A silly smile played on Brooke's lips, and a sense of foreboding zipped along Colin's spine. She faced him, grinning like the cat that'd eaten the last living canary.

"Okay, I'll make a deal with you. I will listen to your sales pitch in its entirety on Tuesday at nine a.m. if you will put on a Santa suit and play Santa for our children's Christmas party right now.

"Me?" he said. Had she gone bonkers since college? "You know I think Santa is hoax created by the toy companies. I hate Christmas."

She shrugged. "Look. We have a children's party scheduled in fifteen minutes and our Santa showed up drunk. I need a Santa."

He shook his head, knowing instinctively this wasn't a good idea, yet he needed this sale.

"You want an appointment to show me your product. I'll listen to your spiel if you play Santa for one afternoon."

Colin took a deep breath and exhaled. He'd targeted six hospitals and needed at least four of them to purchase the product in order to beat Logan. This hospital was one of his must-sell-or-be-left-behind' locations. If wearing a Santa suit for a couple of hours got his foot in the door, he could do it. All he would have to do is listen to whiny kids tell him their wishes.

But what could he get out of the deal besides a chance to show Brooke his product? And she clearly was resist to purchasing from Colin McDermott.

"Who are the decision makers in this hospital?" he asked.

Brooke looked at him strangely as she told him the names of the people who decided on major purchases.

"If I do this for you, you'll guarantee at least three of

them will attend the meeting, including the head of pharmacy."

She contemplated him for a long moment before she turned and glanced at the woman standing in the doorway like she intended to refuse Colin. Finally she turned back toward him. "I can't guarantee their presence, but I'll ask them."

"How will I know you asked them?" he questioned. He needed some guarantees.

"If they can't attend the meeting, I will give you their cards, and you can contact them directly."

That seemed fair enough. At least he would know who to contact when she said no. He sighed. "So what do I have to do when I play Santa?"

A confident grin spread across her face, and Colin knew she thought she'd won this interaction. But he'd at least gotten an appointment, and that was all he needed to make a sale. He'd gotten screwed into playing Santa, but he'd win the grand prize.

Even if he had to wear a Santa suit to do it.

Chapter Two

How difficult could it be to play Santa? Colin thought, stepping into the red wool suit in the ugly green hospital bathroom. The wool reeked of moth balls and the pillow they'd given him to stuff under the coat made his stomach appear like a square block of fat. He tried to punch it into a round ball, which only made it worse.

When he sold the hospital on his software program and won the promotion, the time spent faking jolly old Saint Nick would pay off. An afternoon spent looking like a fool and listening to children whine about what they deserved for Christmas could put him in California running the western division.

The hospital speaker system paged a doctor while Colin belted the loose-fitting pants snug. Last he attached the beard, the wig, and finally the hat. He glanced in the mirror at his image and the memory of sitting on Santa's lap as a young boy hit him square in the chest. His stomach roiled with the memory. He took a deep breath to release the tension in his neck and control the rapid beating of his heart.

Colin hated Christmas. Yet here he stood in a Santa suit staring at his reflection in the mirror, wondering how in the hell he'd gotten in this predicament.

He adjusted the beard, gave the hat a cocky tilt, and gazed one last time in the mirror. He appeared at least eighty. "Showtime! This is for the prize. Colin McDermott, western sales director. Go get 'em, Tiger."

Colin yanked open the door of the restroom and stepped into the hall where nurses, lab technicians and doctors passed him. Amelia stood waiting for him, an anxious grimace on her face.

"Ready?"

"Yes," he said and followed her down a hall past a

nurses' station.

People stared at him. Some smiled and called, "Merry Christmas."

He nodded. If they only knew he was a top-notch Grinch and wanted to shout "Bah, humbug!" at the top of his lungs.

Finally they reached a set of double doors, where she halted.

"Okay, remember all you do is listen to the children's wishes. Most of their parents can't afford what they're asking for, so don't promise anything. Each child gets a picture taken with Santa. Smile and say Merry Christmas." She took a deep breath, paused for a moment, and inspected him. "Any questions?"

He laughed. "Piece of cake."

When she smiled, the tension eased in her face. "Thanks, we were desperate for a Santa."

"Yeah, I know," he said. Brooke didn't know about his past, but she knew he thought Christmas was a merchandising hoax.

Colin opened the door and thirty smiling, scared, shy faces greeted him. A cheer rose from the kids, but some were more subdued. Some children wore street clothes, but many wore hospital gowns. A few took one look at him and buried their faces in their mother's legs, clearly afraid.

What could go wrong? They were kids. In a matter of minutes he'd hear their requests and be out the door with his appointment secured, never to play Santa again.

"Ho, ho, ho," he said, the sound weak, so he tried again. "Ho, ho, ho. Who wants to sit on Santa's lap and tell me what they want for Christmas?"

A line quickly formed as Colin walked over to a chair. Amanda hurried to his side. "Not that chair, Santa. This one here where the kids can see you."

Colin laughed and walked to a chair in the middle of

the room. As he sat, the wig slipped down over his eye and the older children snickered. He pushed it back into place and glanced at the first child.

A robust seven- or eight-year-old in street clothes hopped onto his lap, and Colin released a grunt as the weight of the kid hit his legs.

"What's your name?"

"Charles Rayburn the third and I want a Wii for Christmas," the boy said, not in the least shy.

"Have you been a good boy this year, Charles?"

The boy frowned. "I think so, but my mom says you're going to put coal in my stocking. If you bring me coal, next year when I sit on your lap, I'll pee on you."

"What?" Colin said, not certain that he'd heard the child correctly. Had this kid just threatened to pee on him? Crap, what was he doing here? He had sales to make, not time to listen to threats from a child.

The little boy dropped his voice. "Look, I just want a Wii game so I can beat all my friends when we play. If you could help me out, next year I'll be extra good."

Colin leaned into the boy so that very few heard him. "Mind your mother or get a job if you want a Wii. Threatening Santa doesn't get you what you want."

The boy's eyes widened at his tone.

"Look into the camera, smile and say Merry Christmas."

The kid obeyed, and when he jumped off Colin's lap, he glanced back in surprise at Santa before moving away.

"Next," Santa called. How long would it take him to listen to these kids? If this is what he could expect, the appointment should have every board member attending. After this, the hospital should be begging him to let them buy his software.

The next kid wanted a bike, and the next a baby doll, a G.I. JOE, a Play Station 3, and then came the crybaby. No matter what he said, the little girl sat on his lap and cried. Her mother tried everything to shut her up so they could at least take a picture. Finally, Colin reached his screaming limit.

"Sweetie, look into the camera, smile and I'll give you five dollars to shut up and get off my lap."

The little girl's eyes widened in disbelief, but the tears stopped. After the click of the camera, she jumped down and turned back expectantly. Colin reached into his pocket and slipped her a five. She smiled and walked away while he watched her, dumbfounded.

After the children saw Santa, they were given a small stocking filled with crayons and a coloring book on safety during the holidays.

Three kids later, they put a six-month-old baby on his lap. Colin held the squirming child and sighed with relief. At least this one appeared happy as the baby cooed and reached for his beard. Colin tried to turn the child toward the camera for the photo. A weird gurgle erupted from the baby, and he spewed burp toward him faster than Colin could dodge. The mess landed on his chest. A milky, sour substance that smelled like someone had left the milk jug in the refrigerator long past the due date overwhelmed him. God, it stank!

Amelia ran to him, a rag in her hand, her eyes wide with horror. "Oh no, not the suit."

She scrubbed his chest, trying to get the burp off the furry lapel.

"What about me, lady?" he asked, seething beneath the beard.

Amelia tried not to laugh as she smiled at him. "Sorry, but the suit is borrowed," she said, in a low whisper. "I've got to return it tonight."

The next little girl gave him a big smile, hopped up on his lap and stared at him with large, emerald eyes that twinkled with merriment.

"Merry Christmas," he said, a little wary. What could happen next?

"You haven't done this much have you?" the child said, looking at him as if she could see beneath the beard and the wig.

"What makes you say that?" he asked.

"Santa doesn't hand out money. And you got kind of mad at that baby," she said quietly.

He leaned in closer to her. "That little girl wouldn't stop crying. She was getting on my nerves. Even Santa can only take so much crying. Believe me, tears don't get you what you want. And baby burp? Come on, it stinks."

The little girl laughed, her giggle somehow contagious, and he couldn't help but smile.

"What's your name?" he asked.

"Olivia."

"What do you want for Christmas, Olivia?"

"I want a puppy," she said, with a shake of her honey curls.

"That sounds like a reasonable request," he said, nodding his Santa-disguised head in agreement.

The little girl frowned. "Yeah, I thought so, but my Mom says I can't have one. She says that we don't have a house, and dogs need a yard."

"What about a little dog?"

"I know, but I think she just doesn't want a dog. So that's why I'm asking you," the child said. "I know you'll bring me a puppy."

He was in so much trouble. How did he get out of this without promising her something he couldn't deliver?

"Your Mom and Dad have to approve all your Santa gifts," Colin said, trying not to cross the boundaries.

She stuck her lower lip out and frowned, "I don't have a Dad. You're my only hope of getting what I want."

Colin felt a twinge ripple through him. Another child without a father.

He shrugged. "It's okay. I didn't have a father either."

She tilted her head and considered him, her eyes wide. "But you're Santa."

"And you're Olivia. We have something in common."

She laughed at him, and for a moment he couldn't help but smile at this little girl. She was a funny kid.

"So Santa, are you going to bring me a puppy?"

He sighed, wanting to tell the kid yes, knowing in his heart that he would only disappoint her if he did so. "I will send a letter to your Mother and tell her that you've been a very good girl this year and that you deserve a puppy. You have been a good girl, right?"

"Oh yes," she said nodding her head. "I've only gotten the talking-too-much-in-class card twice. And once it wasn't my fault. Michael Shank pulled my hair, and when I turned around to tell him to stop, I got caught."

Colin watched from the corner of his eye as Brooke approached him, a grim look on her face. "Olivia, it's time to go, honey. You're holding up the line."

She frowned. "Mom, Santa is going to send you a letter saying that I have been a really good girl and I deserve a puppy. It can be a small one."

Brooke glared at Colin.

"Is this your daughter?" he asked. The child said she didn't have a father. So what man had gotten Brooke pregnant and never married her? Or had he died a mysterious death? Or had the man just not come home one day?

"Yes, she is," she said in a curt tone. "Come on, Olivia, it's time to go."

"But I haven't had my picture taken with Santa yet."

"Honey, we don't need another Santa picture."

"But I want one. I like this Santa. He's going to get me

a puppy," she insisted.

"I told you, Olivia, that all Santa wishes have to be approved by Mom's and Dad's," Colin said, hoping not to make Brooke angrier.

"And I told you, I don't have a Dad," she said, smartly. "And my Mom doesn't want a dog in the apartment. I need your help."

Brooke placed her hand on her daughter's arm. "Honey, let's just take the picture and move along now so that other kids can get a chance with Santa."

The camera flash caught a pouting Olivia with Santa.

She jumped off Santa's lap. "I want a dog. A small puppy. Don't forget, Santa."

She strode away from Santa and her mother, her blonde curls bouncing. Colin glanced at Brooke. "I didn't know you had a daughter."

"Yes. She's a little stubborn sometimes, so please ignore her."

Colin grinned. "Wonder where she gets that from?"

Brooke frowned and strode away while the next child climbed onto his lap. Only five kids before he could ditch the suit and get back on the road to his next appointment.

~

Brooke's insides were quaking like a nine-point earthquake as she followed her daughter to the hospital's day care center for employee's children. When Brooke had returned to work, she'd felt appreciative that Olivia was close. She checked her in and bent over to give her daughter a good-bye kiss.

"I'll pick you up later."

"I want a puppy for Christmas," she said, with that defiant tone she'd acquired in the last year.

"We'll talk about this when we get home."

Brooke walked out of the day care center, her knees

shaking, her heart racing as the full enormity of what she'd done hit her. At the holiday party, as she'd handed out refreshments and stockings to the children, she'd glanced up to see Olivia sitting on Colin's knee.

The sight of Colin holding Olivia had sent her heart leaping into her throat. She'd had to restrain herself from running over and yanking her baby off his lap.

What the hell had she been thinking to have Colin play Santa when she knew Olivia would be one of the kids he'd see? Now he'd met her daughter.

The past overwhelmed her, and she doubled over as the scene replayed in her mind just like it happened yesterday. Five weeks after the frat party at which someone had spiked the punch, the stick turned blue, indicating she was pregnant with Colin's child.

Scared and frightened, she'd gone to see Colin, to tell him about the baby. But when she asked him how he felt about children, her world tilted even further. He'd told her he never intended to have children.

He didn't want any responsibilities, any commitments that involved kids.

She'd left without telling him about the child she carried.

Stunned, she'd gone home determined to have this baby by herself and never involve Colin. And she had until just about thirty minutes ago, when unbeknownst to him, he'd met his daughter for the first time.

And she'd watched, trying not to react while her heart pummeled inside her chest. Stunned to see their heads bowed together, the way Olivia had Colin's nose and mouth, her green eyes.

Olivia was her daughter. From the moment she'd been born, Brooke had loved Olivia and committed to being the best possible parent she could to make up for the child not having a father.

To this day, it stung that Colin hadn't wanted them. Yet a part of her wondered if she should have told him she was pregnant. But how could she say "Hey, I'm pregnant with your child" after he'd promised he'd never have children? "Oops, sorry you're wrong. You'll be a dad in eight months?"

No, she'd walked out of his apartment and never looked back.

Now her daughter was hers. Colin had rejected the two of them, and they were doing just fine without him.

"Hey, you okay?" Amelia asked as she came around the corner and saw Brooke leaning against the wall. "You're as white as Santa's beard. Sit down here and let me get you some water."

She pushed Brooke into an empty room and sat her in a chair then hurried to a water fountain and returned with a glass. "Are you feeling okay?"

"I'm fine. I think the excitement just got to me is all." No one knew who Olivia's father was, not even her own family. And they would never find out if she could help it.

"Keep drinking that water. You still don't look right," Amelia said. "I was going to your office to tell you thanks for the great Santa. The kids seemed to love him."

"All except for the kid he told to get a job," Brooke said, smiling.

"That was pretty funny. A street-smart kid who threatened Santa," Amelia said. "I was about to step in when he handled it quite well. I don't know where you found him, but he wasn't bad for a first-time Santa. In fact, I hope you can convince him to do the other two times we need a Santa on the floor."

Brooke's insides tightened into a tense knot. She didn't need Colin here on a regular basis and her precocious, troublemaking child to talk to him again and again, possibly rousing his curiosity as to who Olivia's father was.

No, he needed to leave, and *soon.*

"I don't know if that's such a good idea, Amelia. I mean we didn't even think about running a background check on this guy. He could have been a pedophile for all we know. Or into drugs. What have we possibly exposed the children to?"

Her brows drew together in a frown. "I'll run a background check on him before he comes in next time, but you know that I don't leave anyone alone with the children. Not even another parent. There are always at least three adults in the room with them."

"Yes, I know, but he's a sales rep. He probably won't have time to play Santa again," Brooke said, stalling.

Amelia stared at her for a long moment, carefully studying her. "Something's not right. Did you know Colin before he came in today?"

Brooke wondered how she should answer that one and finally decided honesty was the best response. "I knew him in college."

"So why all the comments he could be a pedophile?"

Brooke swallowed and tried not to react to Amelia. "Six years have passed. People change. Or they have dark things in their lives that you don't know about. I'm just looking out for the hospital."

Amelia shook her head. "Nope. I'm not buying this. I don't know what kind of role this guy had in your life, but something tells me you were once close."

"Now you're just trying to weave some kind of story about Colin. If you think he's so hot, why don't you ask him out?" Brooke said, knowing as soon as the words left her mouth, she'd said too much.

She watched her friend's brows rise as she began to laugh.

"I never said I thought he was hot."

Brooke frowned. "Oh."

"But I'm glad to see that somewhere in that mommie persona you wear is a woman alive and well who still recognizes a good-looking man when she sees one." Amelia leaned over and studied her. "So who is this guy?"

She might as well tell her the condensed version. "Someone from a long time ago who had his chance and blew it."

"For some reason I think there's more to this story. But I won't press you until some color returns to your face," Amelia said.

"There's nothing to tell. It's over. I moved on and so has he," Brooke said, rising from the chair Amelia had insisted she fill.

Chapter Three

Two days later Brooke hurried through the hospital, past busy doctors and nurses, on her way to meet her father for lunch. Twice a month they met for a meal, or he would drop by to collect Olivia and take her for a special treat. Her father loved Olivia, and it showed in the way he made time for his granddaughter.

Brooke came around the corner, and her gray-haired father stood waiting. Since her mother had passed, his eyes no longer twinkled with merriment, and his hair gleamed more silver, but slowly he was adjusting to life alone.

"Hi, honey," he said, dropping a kiss on her cheek.

"Hi, Dad," she replied. "How are you?"

"I'm great, but I'll get better," he said with a big smile. "What's on the menu today?"

"Salad bar," she responded. "The same as every week."

He placed his hand on the middle of her back and guided her into the hall toward the cafeteria. "Darn, I hoped some man had convinced you to become a meat-and-potatoes kind of girl."

She glanced over her shoulder at her father and smiled. "Now when do I have time for a man? And what man wants a woman with a five-year-old child that's not his own?"

"A good man," her father responded, holding the cafeteria door open.

"Seen any my age just hanging around?"

He frowned. "I should try to find you someone. You know, like they did in the Middle Ages, when the father bartered the daughter off to a worthy young man."

She shook her head and smiled at her father. "Dad, I think you've got too much time on your hands."

"Louise says you should try Internet dating. As your father, all I can think about are the predators that lurk there."

"Dad, I don't have time," she admitted, not actually interested in going home and looking at profiles of men searching for women.

The cafeteria was noisy today, filled with families, doctors, nurses and hospital staff. They joined the buffet line, and Brooke faced her father. "How is Louise? You two getting married anytime soon?"

He gave a snort. "Louise is a good friend. The idea of leaving the home I shared for so many years with your mother is troubling. This old man doesn't like change. Maybe after we date for a couple of years, but not yet."

Brooke smiled at her widowed father. A year ago, her mother had passed unexpectedly. Recently he'd reconnected with an old high school friend, and they kept one another entertained.

"Whatever you decide, Dad, you know I'm okay with you marrying again."

"I know. But that's a big step. And besides you have very deftly switched the conversation from you to me," he said, his brows rising like she'd been a naughty kid.

She winked at him. "Gotta be quick to keep up with me."

They walked through the line and picked out their food. When they sat at a nearby table, they ate in silence for a few minutes. And then Brooke decided to ask her father the question that recently kept her awake at night.

"Dad, I need to ask you something."

"Anything, sweetheart."

Brooke placed her fork on the table, her appetite gone. "What if Olivia's father walked in one day? What do you think I should do?"

Her father sat silent. "You've always been vague about her father. Your mother and I assumed you met him in college. We hoped you had strong feelings for him.

"I—"

"And if he reappears in your life, only you can decide how much to let him in."

Brooke sighed, picked up her fork, and stabbed her lettuce. "I cared deeply for him, Dad. When I realized I was pregnant, I went to his apartment to tell him. Before I told him my news, he told me kids were not an option. So I left his apartment without ever telling him I was pregnant. Now, I wonder if I did the right thing."

For a moment her father peered at her, then he placed his hand on her arm. "Oh honey, I wish you'd trusted your mother and me with this information when you first learned you were pregnant."

"Why? So that you could have persuaded me to marry him?"

"No, we'd never have forced you to marry anyone. But maybe between the three of us we could have decided if the boy should know about Olivia." His brown eyes beamed with love.

She'd always known her parents loved her regardless that she'd come home from college with a degree in hand and a bun in the oven.

Her father pushed his plate away and leaned toward her. "Sometimes, people say things they don't mean. When Olivia was born, he may have loved her as much as we do. Or he could have confirmed your fears, turned and walked away from the situation. But you didn't give him the opportunity to choose." He took a deep breath and sighed "What's done is done. If he comes back into your life, you'll have to decide if you want him to know his daughter."

Confusion roiled through her. "I was young, Dad. But mainly I was hurt that he didn't want Olivia and me."

"That's understandable. But we don't know for certain that he didn't want you or Olivia."

Now she could see the rationality of what her father said, but she'd been totally freaked out when Colin said he would never have children. She'd packed her bags and run home to the people who loved her.

"You're not mad at me?"

"For what?" he asked. "Olivia is five years old. I thank God every day she's in my life."

"Thanks, Dad," Brooke said, taking a bite of mangled lettuce.

"What prompted this conversation today," her father asked. "Has Olivia's father shown up?"

Brooke stabbed a tomato. "He's not returned in the sense that I'm seeing him, but he did come into the hospital a couple of days ago."

Her father stared at her. "And?"

She shook her head. "All the doubts returned. Maybe I should have given him a chance. Maybe even now I should go to him and say, oh by the way, you have a daughter."

Her father smiled. "Is he married?"

Her pulse skipped for a moment. She hadn't even considered he could be married. But was her father suggesting what she thought? "Dad!"

"Look, I've often thought you weren't over him, and that's why Olivia doesn't have a father."

Brooke had shielded her heart when she'd seen Colin. The pain of carrying his child alone for nine months had built up walls. Yes, they'd only had sex once, but she'd loved him, and it had hurt when Colin admitted he didn't want children. So she'd refused to give him the chance to tell her to rid herself of the baby. That had never been an option.

"Angry and confused is how I felt when I saw him yesterday. Years ago, I loved him. I don't know if he's married. I didn't ask, because it doesn't matter."

"Will you see him again?" he asked.

"Yes."

"Maybe now is the time to figure out once and for all what your feelings are for this man. If you knew, you could move on with your life."

"I know there's no room for him in my life today. You, Olivia, and my job are my life."

~

Tuesday morning Colin arrived at the hospital early to setup his presentation. Before he reached the conference room, Amelia intercepted him, positioning her body in front of the conference door.

"Mr. McDermott, may I have a quick word with you?" she asked.

"Sure," he said. A glance inside showed the decision makers had yet to arrive.

Amelia laid her hand on his arm and smiled, her large blue eyes warm. "Thank you so much for playing Santa last week. I can't tell you how much I appreciate what you did for the children."

"No problem," he said. He tried to step around her, thinking they were done. Her fingers tightened on his arm. Her body blocked the door.

"By playing Santa you're considered a volunteer. I'm unable to pay for your services," she said.

"No problem. Consider it a donation." Again he tried to step around her.

She didn't budge, but rather stepped closer to him.

"I've searched everywhere to find a Santa for our next two parties. It's too late. They all have commitments or are unwilling to donate their time," she said. "I know playing Santa is a huge imposition for you, but you would receive the highest honor of recognition for volunteer service from the hospital if you could help us out. I only need Santa two more times. And you know those volunteer service awards show the board just how important our hospital and the work we do here are to our vendors. Why, the last vendor who volunteered received our largest contract," she rambled on.

Christ, she wanted him to play Santa to a bunch of bratty children again. The little monsters could puke all over him or even worse.

"I'm sorry. I'm in the middle of a big push for year-end sales. I must meet my sales numbers. I can't."

She smiled a sweet, dangerous, arm-twisting grin, her grip locked around his arm, holding him in place.

"I understand. I know your time is very valuable, but think about the children. Who's going to make these sick children smile at Christmas?" she asked, her big, blue, doe eyes sad.

"Can't you get a doctor to volunteer?" he asked.

She shook her head. "Too busy. And the children recognize the doctors. Not hard to miss those eyes that come in and poke you each day."

"I can't." He glanced at his watch. Time was short.

"If you could play Santa, well, I'd be happy to tell the chairman myself and put in a good word for you and your product. I'd tell him how you donated a lot of your precious time to make certain the children of Crystal Mountain General Hospital have a wonderful Christmas party," she said.

He sighed.

"I'd receive a volunteer service award and *your* personal recommendation to the chairman?" he asked.

"Scouts honor," she answered.

He needed this sale. Personal recommendations were worth their weight in gold.

"Only two more times?"

"Yes."

"Okay, I'll do it," he said, already regretting his

decision, anxious to get inside. What the hell was he doing? He didn't have time to play Santa.

On the positive side, he would get to see Brooke again.

"Oh, thank you so much, Colin," she grabbed him and hugged him. "The children will be delighted to learn Santa's coming to the second floor."

"What time?" he asked.

"Three o'clock," she said grinning. She released him and stepped away from the door. "Have a great meeting."

"Now that I can get to it, I will," he said, shaking his head at the way she'd manipulated him.

She smiled that arm-twisting grin one last time in his direction, and he felt like he'd been recruited into active duty.

"Thanks."

Eager to escape, he pushed open the conference room where Brooke stood making coffee.

"Hi." His stomach fluttered at the sight of her. He never became anxious over his presentations. He knew the material and could answer questions with little or no anxiety. But the sight of Brooke's lips turned up in a smile, her green eyes challenging him, had his nerves tap dancing along his spine.

"Hi," she said.

She kept her distance and watched as he set his case on the table. "Do you need anything?"

"A projector screen. The presentation is on my laptop." He quickly removed packets of information from his case. "How many people will attend?"

"Everyone I asked except one. I will give you her business card," she replied.

"Great." He finished his setup with a couple of minutes to spare. He stopped and let his eyes feast on the sight of her. Even after all these years, she could still affect him. Her green sweater-dress clung to her body, and the black ankle boots accentuated her long legs. A moan almost escaped his lips at the memory of those legs wrapped around him.

He pulled a letter from his briefcase and handed it to Brooke.

She looked at it oddly. "What's this?"

"A letter from Santa Claus to you saying what a good girl Olivia is and to please reconsider giving her a puppy."

Brooke rolled her eyes. "Are you kidding me? You want me to show her a letter from Santa to help her get a dog when I told her no?"

"Santa promised Olivia he would send you a letter. If Santa didn't send the letter, she'd be angry the next time she saw him," he responded, not understanding his determination not to disappoint the little girl.

"She's not getting a dog."

"That's between you and her. Santa fulfilled his promise. I'm done." He paused for a second and shook his head. "Well, I thought I was done until the master convincer held me hostage outside the room, finagling me into playing Santa again."

Brooke's eyes widened. "She didn't."

"Oh yes, she did. I need to recruit that girl for sales. Amelia wouldn't let me go until I agreed. So I'm back the next two weeks to play Santa."

"No, you can't."

Colin stopped and studied her. "Why not?"

A frown spread across her forehead, wrinkling her brow. "I don't know, you just can't."

Two people walked into the room and took a seat at the table. Colin turned from Brooke and became centered on business.

He introduced himself and shook hands with the board members as they entered the room.

But as he worked the room, he couldn't help but wonder

at Brooke's reaction to the news he would play Santa again. Why would she care that he'd returned to play the old coot?

~

Brooke grabbed Amelia by the arm, "We need to talk in the cafeteria. Now."

"What's up?" Amelia asked.

They walked into the cafeteria, bought two cups of the stale hospital brew, and sank into chairs. The clank of dishes could be heard in the background as the staff prepared for lunch.

"Why do I get the feeling I've done something that's upset you?" Amelia asked, her eyes questioning.

"Did you ask Colin McDermott to be Santa two more times?"

"Yes, he was a great Santa last week. I haven't been able to find a replacement. It took some arm twisting, but he finally agreed."

Brooke sighed and hung her head. "Oh, God. I didn't want to see him again."

"Why?" Amelia said with a laugh. "Ex-college boyfriend you have a hidden past with? A secret affair?"

Brooke felt the color drain from her face. She swallowed, trying to erase the shock plastered on her face.

"Oh my God," Amelia said, her eyes widening at the realization. "I'm sorry. I have such a big mouth. I never…I never thought…oh, shit."

Brooke shook her head, considering how Amelia could so easily figure it out and how many others would soon realize the truth.

"Damn it, Amelia," Brooke said, her insides locking down, her stomach hard, as fear for her daughter gripped her.

"I'm sorry. I didn't know. I never thought about it until now."

"No one knows, not even my father," Brooke said. "In fact, the only place you could learn the truth was on Olivia's birth certificate. And believe me I've regretted that moment of weakness for years. I wish I'd never listed him."

Amelia shook her head. "I had no idea. Honestly, I just needed someone to play Santa. If I'd known, I would have kept looking and never asked Colin."

Brooke ran her hand over her face. "Do you think you can tell him you've found someone else?"

"I've looked everywhere for a Santa. Now I know why you didn't want him here, but the children won't have a Santa visit unless Colin does it."

Brooke bit her lip. She didn't want him around the hospital, yet he was here today. And if the children didn't see Santa, there was no one to blame but herself.

"I guess there's not much I can do about it now. It's only two more visits. Once Christmas is over, he won't be around any longer. But you are sworn to secrecy as to who is Olivia's father."

Amelia shook her head and leaned forward. "I would never tell anyone. Your secret is safe with me, Brooke."

~

After the presentation, Colin packed his computer and his sales materials, then he glanced around the room, unable to find Brooke.

He went to her office and she wasn't there. Finally, needing some caffeine, he rolled his briefcase into the cafeteria and there she sat nursing a cup of coffee and, talking to Amelia their heads bowed low over the table.

He walked up, and they both jumped.

"Hello there, Santa," Amelia said, a tense smile on her face.

"You need a job in sales. You've got that arm twisting technique down well," he responded.

Her phone chimed, and she hopped up from the chair. "Oops, gotta run. That's my signal that I have a conference call in ten minutes." She smiled at him. "Bye, Santa."

Colin slid into her vacated chair. "Why don't you want me to play Santa?"

"I don't care." Brooke shrugged her shoulders, but the tense lines around her mouth said otherwise.

He watched as she tried to act like it meant nothing, but her frown and flashing green eyes belied her words.

"I thought you were too busy. And you didn't seem thrilled about playing the role the other day," she finally said.

"I wasn't. But Amelia pretty much held me hostage until I agreed by promising me all kinds of volunteer awards."

Brooke laughed a little. "Yes, she's good at getting what she wants."

"How do you think the presentation went?"

She nodded. "Good."

"Do you think they'll buy the software?"

"It's not my decision," Brooke said, glancing around the cafeteria.

"But you have influence with the board."

"Some, yes."

"Can I count on your support?" he asked.

Brooke pursed her lips. God, he remembered kissing those full lips, and a zing of awareness shot through him. What happened to them? Together in college they'd had fun. They'd laughed and played and studied and had one night of sex.

"I don't know. I need to run the numbers to see if we can even afford your program," she said.

He nodded. "Fair enough. The software is not cheap. But it's well worth the price. "

She didn't say anything, and he couldn't stand not

knowing any longer. Her emerald eyes warmed him and her gentle nature always soothed him.

"What happened between us, Brooke? I thought we had a good thing, and then suddenly you disappeared. You didn't even say good-bye," he said, watching her. He clutched his coffee cup, his fingers white with tension.

Her forehead wrinkled in a frown before she glanced away. "We were young. I needed to go home."

"What called you home so suddenly that you couldn't spare me a five-minute phone call?"

"I finished my exams and I left."

He leaned toward her and studied her hand. "When did you get married? I don't see a wedding band."

Her eyes widened as she rose from her chair. "I need to get back to work. Why don't you call me in a week, and I'll let you know the progress and where we stand on our decision."

Colin stood and ignored her comment. "I see no wedding band, so I don't think you're married."

She hurried to the elevator, and he strode after her. At the door, she turned to face him. "It's been great to see you again. Good-bye, Colin."

Disappointment surged through Colin, and he frowned as she stepped onto a waiting elevator. The doors closed, and he wondered at her reaction. She never answered what had called her home so suddenly. What was she hiding?

Chapter Four

Three days later Colin once again stood in the hospital bathroom, slipping on the despised Santa suit. He'd spent the morning giving a second sales presentation at another hospital and had an appointment at a third scheduled for Monday morning.

Staying at a local hotel, he should be moving on down the road, but so far he'd remained here in Crystal Mountain. Mainly because he wanted the sale to Brooke's hospital, and also it was a good place to make quick day trips to other regional hospitals.

And yet it was fifteen days before Christmas and he didn't have a single sale. People were more interested in holiday decorations, baking cookies, and swigging eggnog than purchasing software.

Dressing like this old geezer had better get him the sale.

He pulled on the beard and wig, placing the hat at a cockeyed angle atop his head. "Ho, ho, ho, you little rug rats. You better be nice, or I'll put coal in all your stockings."

He took a deep breath and knew he couldn't procrastinate any longer. *Smile, McDermott. Its show time.*

Con the children into believing he was Santa, and he'd win the software sale. He had to continue envisioning his Santa act this way, or he'd run out of this hospital screaming in a suit he hated.

He opened the door of the men's room, and Brooke stood waiting for him.

"Ho, ho, ho," he said. "Merry Christmas."

"Knock it off, Santa," she said to him, clearly pissed. She blocked his path, her arms crossed, fury sparking her green eyes. "If Olivia is there this afternoon, do not mention the puppy or the letter."

"You didn't give her the letter, did you?" he said

calmly.

"I—I, oh it's none of your business. She's my daughter."

Colin shook his head. "I don't know kids very well, but your daughter seemed bright, and if she sees Santa, she's going to want to know why I didn't send her mommy the letter." Anger surged through him like a power charge. Brooke had placed him in an awkward situation. "I'm not lying for you. If she asks me, I'll tell her the truth, that I gave you the letter."

He moved past her and began to walk down the hall. This whole situation sucked tremendously, and he was tired of dealing with Brooke. She'd wanted to rid the hospital of him, and she'd lied to him, yet he couldn't be too mean, because she was one of the decision makers for the board.

"You wouldn't dare," she said, catching up to him.

"I'm not lying to your daughter," he said. "You know if she sees me, she'll ask about the letter."

"Then I'm not going to let her see Santa."

He laughed. "Not a problem."

They arrived at the door and he heard children laughing. Today he was on the floor where children with serious conditions like cancer and leukemia were treated. These children had life-threatening illnesses, and he intended to give them the Santa they deserved, even if he did hate having to play this role.

"Crap," Brooke said, glancing through the window in the door. "She's already in there."

He peered at Brooke. "I have to go in and be jolly and happy and try to make these sick children's day just a little better. If you don't want Olivia to know that I gave you the letter, you better get her out of there. Excuse me," he said and walked through the door, leaving her standing in the hall.

"Santa!" the children cried as Colin strolled in. Their

reception filled him with warmth. They were happy to see him, and even though many faced life-threatening illnesses, they had smiles on their faces.

"Ho, ho, ho, Merry Christmas everyone," he called and gave them each a genuine smile. No matter how crappy his day, these children had endured worse. He may hate playing Santa, but he'd be the best damn Santa he could be for them.

"Who wants to tell me what they want for Christmas?" he asked, sitting down in a chair.

Amelia beamed at him, and he relaxed.

A timid little girl of seven approached him, and he picked her up and put her on his lap. "What's your name?"

"Emma," she said softly.

"Tell Santa what I can bring you for Christmas."

She gazed at her hands, twisting them in her lap. Finally, she raised the prettiest blue eyes and looked at him earnestly. Her voice whisper soft, she said, "I want my mommy to have a new dress."

Colin sat stunned. He hadn't expected this request. "Honey, I'm here for *you*. Tell me what *you* want."

She shook her head. "I don't need anything. I have my baby but my mommy never gets anything, because all our money goes to help me get well. So I want her to have a new dress."

A lump expanded in Colin's throat, and he swallowed to force it down. "Is your mommy here in the room?" he asked.

"Yes, that's her next to Miss Amelia."

"What's her name?" he asked.

"Sara Bronson," she whispered.

Colin nodded. "Okay, I'll do everything I can to make certain she gets a new dress."

The little girl reached up and hugged his neck. "Thank you, Santa." And then in an even lower voice she said,

"She likes blue."

"I'll remember blue," he said, his voice cracking.

He helped her off his lap and sat speechless at the way the child had wrenched his heart out of his chest.

The child wanted to sacrifice her gift for her mother. He swallowed the tears clogging his throat. Children didn't deserve this kind of crap.

A little boy approached him.

"Hey, Santa," he said.

"Hey, little man. What can I do for you?"

The boy thought for a moment. "I want a new bike so that when I get out of here, I can ride it around my neighborhood."

"What kind of bike? Any particular style?"

"A ten-speed."

"Aren't you a little young for a ten-speed bike?"

"No, my big brother has one, and I want to ride with him."

"I will put it on the list."

"Thanks," he said and jumped off his lap.

The next three kids had similar requests for toys ranging from video games to computers.

This floor and these kids were different from his first experience. A growing sense of pain riddled him. It was one thing to see an adult with no hair, but seeing a five-year-old little girl with a bald head and bright smile ripped him apart. Then the kid with the missing leg was like icing on the bad-feeling cake.

At the end of the hour, Olivia stood before him.

"Hi, Santa," she said with a big, bright smile.

"Hi Olivia," he replied. Her blonde curls and emerald eyes reminded him of Brooke, and he wondered if she had looked like this at Olivia's age.

She climbed onto his lap and whispered low. "I'm not supposed to be here, but I wanted to see you."

He whispered back, "But when you do something your Mom says you're not supposed to do, isn't that being bad?"

She frowned. "I had to talk to you."

"About what?" he asked, already knowing the answer.

"Have you mailed the letter?" she asked.

"Yes," he replied, wondering how he could minimize the damage.

She frowned. "Mommy hasn't received it."

"Well, maybe it hasn't come in the mail yet. The post office is kind of busy this time of year."

She perked up. "Oh. You're probably right."

He thought for a long moment on how to help Brooke. He didn't want to disappoint Olivia, but he also could see Brooke's side. "Olivia, sometimes we don't always get what we want."

"Yeah, I know."

"Look around you. All these children did not want to get sick. They didn't want to spend Christmas in the hospital. They want to be home with their families or any place besides here."

She nodded her head. "I know." She leaned forward. "Some of them will die. I know because last year one of the kids wasn't here for Christmas."

"That's really sad."

"Uh-huh."

"It may not be the right time for you to get a puppy."

She shook her head, "No. I want a puppy or a little sister."

He laughed out loud. "You need a daddy before you can have a little sister."

She frowned at him. "No, you're wrong. I don't have a daddy." She gave him a surprised look. "Santa, you don't know everything."

He grinned at her. "You are so right, Olivia. Santa doesn't know everything.

She jumped down from his lap. "I'm going to tell my mommy to watch for your letter."

She flounced off, and he from her self-confident swagger, he knew she was more determined than ever to get what she wanted.

Colin watched her go and wondered. Who was Olivia's father? She was maybe, five years old. They'd been out of college for six years, which meant she had to have been conceived right after college. But who had Brooke been seeing after she left town?

~

When all the children had seen Santa, he watched them wheel themselves down the hall to their rooms. He couldn't leave until the last child left with a piece of candy and the promise of a better tomorrow.

The first time he'd played Santa had been difficult, because the last place he dreamed of being was at the children's ward in a Santa suit. But this time, even though he didn't want to be there, just one look at these children and he'd forgotten about his problems, and wanted to put smiles on their faces.

Sometimes life sucked even for children.

These were the children that Christmas had forgotten. These were the children for whom waking each morning meant they were here for one more day. That in itself was a gift. And he wanted to make their time with Santa special.

He walked down the hall toward the men's room where he could change back into his street clothes and give the Santa suit back to Amelia. He only had to do this one more time before he could get his accommodation, though that no longer seemed as relevant.

As he rounded the corner, he stopped. Logan stood talking to Brooke. Crap! He wanted to turn and walk away, but he needed to change his clothes and leave for his next appointment.

Brooke said something, and Logan whirled around and saw him. In less than a minute, his eyes widened and he started to laugh. He pulled out his cell phone and took a picture.

Christ! Now the whole office would know about him playing Santa. His tough guy image would suffer.

"I couldn't believe it when I heard you were the new hospital Santa. No wonder you haven't made any sales, Colin. You're too busy playing Santa," he said with a wicked grin.

"Ho, ho, ho, asshole," he said. "This suit is bringing me good luck."

"Have you made the sale yet?" Logan asked.

Colin glanced at Brooke, who ignored the two men. "No."

"Then the suit might not be working for you." Logan looked him up and down. "Man, I never would have believed it if I hadn't seen it with my own eyes. Jolly ole Saint Colin."

All the good will Colin felt from the children suddenly seemed like an ankle chain holding him back. What the hell was he doing? Everything he'd worked so hard toward was in jeopardy because of this jerk, and Colin was busy playing bleeding-heart Santa to a bunch of sick kids instead of beating the pavement.

"If you're here to try to present to the board, you're too late. I've already shown them the product, and we're waiting on a decision."

Logan smiled. "Yeah, I heard. But it was worth the trip down here just to see you wasting your time in a Santa outfit. I'll be sure to blow up the picture and post it on the bulletin board for everyone to see," he said.

"Just as long as you put *western sales director* beneath the picture that will be fine," Colin said. "I'll be sure to put something besides coal in your stocking this year."

"No need. Santa is bringing me the promotion. Good luck pitching the product to all the kiddies on your lap. I'll be out making sales while you suck up to the kids," he said as he walked away.

Colin stood motionless while Brooke shook her head at him. "Western sales director," she drawled out slowly. "No wonder you're trying so hard to sell your product to our hospital."

All the frustration of the last week seemed to spill from him in a torrent. "I worked hard all year, and I was the number one sales rep until last month. He sneaks up on me with a huge account that brought our sales to within one hundred dollars of each other. So now instead of the job being handed to me, I have to earn it all over again. So yeah, I'm out trying hard to sell several hospitals before December 23 when the contest is over and the new sales director will be flown to beautiful warm, California. And this," he said pointing to the suit, "isn't exactly how you make sales."

Brooke smiled. "No, but it is one way to impress the board members. Sacrifice of one's self is always a good quality in a hospital. Helping others and making people happy, that's more important than a sale. So smile Santa, and you might use this same tactic at your next appointment."

He sighed. "Ho, friggin' ho, ho."

~

Brooke walked away from Colin and couldn't keep from chuckling. When the salesman from the same company had shown up asking to make an appointment with her, she'd been surprised.

When she'd told him that Colin had already shown the product and was in fact coming down the hall at that moment, he'd been stunned. The energy flowing between the two men and the blatant competition had been startling.

The air had fairly crackled with tension. Yet Colin never appeared angry, but rather laid back like a cat ready to pounce for the kill.

She admired the way he'd handled Logan. The other man had seemed crass. Even before Colin had shown up, she'd been ready to show him the door.

Brooke reached her office and walked in. She sank into the chair, staring at the work piled on her desk. She needed to work today as tomorrow she was taking her father to the VA hospital in Denver. It would be an all day trip for him to have some dental work done under anesthesia.

She picked up Olivia's letter from Santa. She didn't want to give this to Olivia, but what choice did she have? The child expected a letter from Santa.

Colin's reappearance in her life over a week ago had created nothing but problems and distractions. Including the fact she still wanted to pull him into her arms and meld her lips to his. Becoming involved with him again could be dangerous not only to her heart, but also the fact he could learn Olivia was his daughter.

They'd been so young when she'd gotten pregnant, but she wouldn't change a thing. She loved Olivia with all her heart.

She picked up the letter from Santa. Her daughter wanted a puppy, and the thought of a dog that would require training, cleaning, feeding, and attention was just too much to add into her stressed world right now. Taking care of Olivia and working forty hours a week was more than she could handle. The thought of a dog was tiring.

Yet, her daughter would be heartbroken if Santa didn't bring her a dog. What was she to do?

~

The next day Amelia glanced up at the knock on her door. Colin McDermott stood in the doorway.

"Hey, I thought I'd drop by to see if you've put in that commendation for volunteer of the year yet?" he said, teasing.

She smiled, knowing he meant every word. "I've got the paperwork somewhere here on my desk to send up to the chairman's office."

"Do you need some help completing the form?" he asked. "After all, I've played Santa twice for you."

She shook her head. "You really do want that sale, don't you?"

"I need it if I'm going to win this promotion," he said, leaning against the doorway. "Have you seen Brooke anywhere?"

"She took the day off to take her father to the VA hospital in Denver. They should return before five."

He frowned, the disappointment evident on his face. "Oh well, I'll catch her when I return. I'm getting ready to head out to Montana for a few days and wanted to speak with her before I left."

"I'll tell Brooke you stopped by. Be careful. Remember, you're scheduled to play Santa again next week."

"Yeah, how could I forget," he said. He checked his watch. "I better go if I'm going to make it down the road before it gets too dark. Talk to you soon."

She watched Colin walk out the door and wondered about him. Brooke had not given her any details about this man being Olivia's father. Only her face had given her secret away. So what had happened between the two of them to make Brooke keep her pregnancy a secret?

Either way, it wasn't her concern. She needed to forget that he was Olivia's father and concentrate on how she was going to raise money for the hospital.

She glanced at her notes, trying to decide what her next

fundraiser would be after the holidays. She usually presented the board with a full year's worth of fundraising activities in January, and this year she just felt burned out. What else could she do?

The phone rang and Amelia picked up the receiver.

"This is Hope Bolton in the ER. Do you know where Brooke is?" she asked.

"She took the day off to take her father for some medical procedure at the VA hospital. Why?"

"There's been a bus accident and Olivia is seriously injured. She's down in the ER."

"Oh my God. I'm on my way."

Amelia sprang out of her chair and ran down the hallway. When she reached the ER, she stopped at the sight of total chaos. Wall-to-wall stretchers filled with children lined the floor, anxious parents at their sides.

She found Hope. "Have you tried Brooke's cell phone?"

"Yes, no answer. I tried her father's number. No answer. Are there any other nearby relatives who would have the authority to okay treatment?"

"Not that I know of." Amelia stopped, suddenly remembering the conversation regarding Colin. He was here in the hospital, about to leave on a road trip.

But she didn't have the right to tell Colin he was the girl's father.

"Where is she?"

The nurse pointed to an examining room. Through the window, she could see a doctor frantically working. "It looks like her spleen is ruptured and she's bleeding into her abdomen. She's going into shock and we need to get her to surgery."

Amelia glanced at the nurse. "But you can't do surgery until you hear from Brooke."

The nurse shook her head. "Every minute is crucial."

Oh God, what should she do? Brooke had confided in

her that Colin was listed as the father on Olivia's birth certificate. He was here in the hospital, but she didn't have the right to tell him about Olivia. Only Brooke should tell him the truth. But could they wait until Brooke returned? What if even now, Colin was walking out the hospital door?

"You and I both know how spotty the phone reception can be between here and Denver. And if they're in the hospital, her phone may be turned off. I don't know."

"Geez," the nurse said.

An alarm on one of the machines hooked up to Olivia began to wail.

"She's coding," the nurse said.

The doctor immediately started yelling to start compressions on Olivia's chest. The child didn't move.

"Page Colin McDermott," Amelia said her voice shaking. "Page him *now*."

"Santa?"

"Yes, Santa," Amelia said watching as the team managed to get Olivia's heart going again. She couldn't let Olivia die. Brooke would have to understand. She had no choice but to tell Colin he was Olivia's father.

Chapter Five

Gabriella appeared in the small emergency room, watching as gurney after gurney was wheeled in with an injured kid. The room echoed with crying children as their parents stood by, their faces anxious and scared. Devon stood in the corner, grinning as he watched her approach, igniting feelings that she'd learned long ago to keep under control.

She walked over to him, doubled up her fist and punched him on the arm. Well maybe she still needed to learn to control some of those feelings.

He jumped back. "What are you doing? You can't do that. It's against the rules."

"So fire me!" she said, crossing her arms over her chest to keep her fists under control.

"If only I could."

"It felt good to try to knock some sense into you."

He smiled. "Well, I didn't feel a thing."

"Of course, you didn't. You have no heart. No soul. Anyone that would crash a busload of children is pure evil."

"That's my game plan. I warned you I wouldn't play nice on this case," he said, leaning against the wall of the hospital emergency room, smiling and watching the chaos he'd created.

"Injuring children is the lowest vile act. You've made me so angry that I'm more determined than ever to save Colin McDermott," Gabriella said, observing the trauma with horror.

"Well, you better put on your seat belt, because the ride is about to become bumpy," Devon said with a smile, obviously satisfied with the destruction he'd created.

"What have you done?" she asked, putting her hands on her hips as she glared at him.

"I'm just setting Colin up so he'll run," Devon said. "He never wanted children, and yet he has a daughter he knows nothing about. Until now."

Devon pointed to an examining room where a medical team bustled about, working on a small child. Gabriella looked into the room.

"Oh Devon, you've hurt so many innocent children in your need to reach quota," Gabriella said. She vaporized through the wall, reaching Olivia. She ran her fingers down the girl's arm, picking up her little hand. Gabriella held it between her fingers. "It's okay, sweetie, you're not alone. I'm not going to let anything bad happen to you."

The child didn't stir. Her eyes remained closed. Doctors and nurses surrounded Olivia.

Devon appeared inside the room. "She's not looking too good."

"You're using her to get to her father. That's just not right," Gabriella said, running a hand through Olivia's hair.

"Check her vitals," a doctor called out to the team.

Gabriella stood invisible amongst them, holding the little girl's hand.

"We need to get her to surgery," the doctor called.

"Devon, get out of my sight. You've done enough damage."

"Okay, but the fireworks haven't started yet. I'll be close by, watching," he said, laughing as he vaporized from the room.

Gabriella squeezed the little girl's hand. "It's okay, I'm here with you."

~

Colin was walking through the reception area of the hospital, on his way out the door when he heard his name across the speaker.

"Paging Colin McDermott to the emergency room. Mr. McDermott, please go to the emergency room."

It couldn't be for him. He didn't know anyone in the emergency room. Who could need him in the emergency room?

Still, he made his way toward that area of the hospital. Unease trickled down his spine as he went to the one place in the hospital he avoided. Too much drama in this section of the hospital for a salesman.

As Colin rounded the corner into the crowded waiting area of the emergency room, the place was packed with injured kids. God, this looked bad! Children lay on gurneys in the hallway, anxious adults by their side. Some were crying, and some watched, their eyes wide with fright, as doctors and nurses rushed about.

Amelia stood scanning the room, searching for him. He walked up to her.

"Did you page me?" he asked, hoping that she wasn't going to ask him to put that stupid Santa suit on and try to cheer these children up.

"Thank God you hadn't left yet. I need your help," she said, taking his arm and hurrying him down a hall.

"I don't have time to play Santa today," he said, confused, as Amelia pulled him down a hallway. She stopped in front of a room.

"What's going on? Who's in there?" he asked, staring into the narrow glass window. The realization that it was Olivia smacked him upside the head. He liked that little girl, and there she lay on a bed with a team of doctors and nurses working on her.

"Olivia's been hurt. Brooke is off today. The hospital needs a family member to sign the consent form for Olivia to have surgery."

He stared at her wondering why she was asking him. "I'm not family…"

His voice trailed off, and like a jolt from a lightning bolt, he realized the time frame between when Brooke had left college to the time that Olivia had been born.

Oh my God.

Amelia grimaced. "It's not my place to tell you this, but we have to get her into surgery. Your name is listed on the birth certificate as the father. You can sign the consent."

The world around him seemed to spin away, and everything from the past suddenly made sense. Brooke had come to see him that day because she was pregnant.

Olivia was his daughter? He had a child? Something he'd sworn he'd never have. A child. And she lay dying.

He had a daughter.

Amelia's voice seemed to ebb and flow inside his head, and while he heard her, his brain moved in slow motion.

"Olivia was born here. I've already had administration verify the records. I can show you the actual birth certificate listing you as the father. Will you sign the consent form?"

The doctor came out of the examining room. "Have we found the mother yet?"

"No, but I've got the father right here," Amelia said.

"Dr. Egbert," he said, shaking Colin's hand. "Your daughter has a ruptured spleen. She's in shock from the trauma and blood loss. They're preparing an operating room now. Do we have your consent to operate?"

A nurse appeared beside him with paperwork for him to sign. Colin stood there in a daze. He had a daughter. A daughter that needed surgery, and Brooke couldn't be found.

"Have you tried to reach her mother again?" he asked.

"I keep calling every few minutes," the nurse said.

"We can't wait," the doctor told him. "We need to go now. She's already crashed once."

What choice did he have? He wasn't going to sit back and watch Olivia die.

He reached for the paperwork and signed while the doctor motioned for the medical team to take her up. "We'll be in surgery about an hour. The nurse will show you where to wait."

Colin watched as the medical team wheeled a pale, unconscious Olivia from the examining room. The doctor followed close behind as they hurried to the elevator.

Amelia looked at Colin. "Are you okay? You look a little white."

He watched the medical team enter the elevator with his daughter's limp body. *His daughter.*

He ignored Amelia, leaned against the wall, put his head in his hands. Shock held him hostage as the words reverberated through his head. She was his daughter. He had a child, something he'd sworn he'd never have. A child, and she was dying.

A daughter. And she'd spent the first five years of her life without a father. Just like he'd spent ten years of his childhood without his mother or father.

History had repeated itself even though he'd done his best to keep that from happening. Another child left with only one parent.

Damn!

He thought back to the last time in college he'd seen Brooke. Right before graduation, she'd come to his apartment and asked him all kinds of questions. She'd asked him how he felt about children and he'd been bluntly honest. He didn't want kids.

Colin had never explained about his childhood or given her any reason for his feelings. She must have been pregnant at the time.

Obviously, he'd screwed up. Everyone messed up sometimes. But he'd messed up royally by never realizing the truth. Brooke had left college pregnant with his child.

He didn't want to risk leaving a child without its parents. He didn't want a child to experience the heartbreak of how it felt to not be wanted. To wait for days, weeks, months, and years for your mother to return only to slowly realize she was never coming back.

To this day, he'd never seen or heard from his mother. Maybe she was dead, or maybe she was just a deadbeat mom who didn't want her son. Whatever had happened, she'd left him alone. And he'd never wanted that to happen to a child of his.

What did he do now?

Damn, he didn't want children, but he didn't want Olivia to die.

~

"Oh, Devon, where are you? I know you're hiding around here somewhere," Gabriella called.

Devon appeared before her, his arms crossed, frowning.

"I just wanted to be the first to tell you that Colin signed the paperwork," Gabriella said with a smile. "He's in the waiting room waiting for the surgeon. He hasn't run yet."

Devon sighed. "So it didn't exactly work out like I'd hoped, but that doesn't mean I'm through with him. Once the child is well, he'll run, just you wait and see."

Gabriella laughed. "I'm not so certain. He didn't want children because he didn't want another child to face the kind of uncertainty he grew up with. Now that he knows he has a child, he's going to take care of her."

Devon laughed. "Dream on, Gabriella. You always expect the best out of these humans, but we both know they can do evil."

"Not unlike you," she said with a sarcastic edge. "Because of your heinous act, I must comfort the other families whose children are hurt. One day soon, it's going to so suck to be you."

"Oohhh, I'm scared."

"You should be."

Gabriella disappeared into the waiting room, where anxious parents waited for news of their injured children. Touching them each on the shoulder, she whispered words of encouragement in their ears.

They couldn't see her, but she gave each of them the support they so very much needed.

~

Brooke drove out of the mountain range and into the valley where the town of Crystal Mountain lay nestled between towering pines and rocks. Her father dozed beside her, a result of the anesthesia during the procedure. The dentist had implanted a new bridge, and though her father wasn't in pain, the meds left him drowsy.

Just as the car topped the other side of the mountain pass, her phone beeped. She glanced down at the phone sitting in the cradle and saw she had five new messages and multiple calls. She hit her Bluetooth to play her messages.

"This is Hope Bolton, the nurse in the Crystal Mountain General Hospital ER. Please call me as soon as you receive this message."

Why would the nurse from the ER be calling her? Unless something was wrong with Olivia.

She hit the next one.

"Hey, it's Amelia, call me."

"This is Hope Bolton again, I need to speak to you."

Oh God, something was wrong. She called the hospital ER.

"This is Brooke Warren, I need to speak to Hope Bolton."

The nurse came on the line. "Brooke?"

"What's wrong, Hope?"

"Where are you?"

"I'm about thirty minutes from the hospital? Why? Is something wrong?"

"The daycare bus was involved in an accident. Olivia was injured."

Gut wrenching terror gripped her, and for a moment she feared she would drive off the road. "No," she wailed. "Is she okay?"

"Are you driving?"

"Yes."

"Brooke I need you to focus on the road. Getting into an accident is not going to help her. Just get here as quick as you can. She's in the operating room."

"Surgery? What's wrong with her?"

"She took a bad blow to the abdomen that ruptured her spleen. She was rushed into surgery so the doctor could remove it and stop the bleeding."

"Is she going to be okay?"

"The surgery should repair the damage. Just get here safely."

The nurse ended the call, and Brooke's hands shook on the steering wheel. A sob escaped.

Her father jerked awake.

"What's wrong?" her dad asked.

"Olivia's school bus was in an accident. She's at the hospital. She's been taken into surgery."

"Oh my God, is she okay?"

"The nurse seemed to think she was going to be okay."

Tears started to flow down Brooke's cheeks. "We've got to get to Olivia."

"Honey, take a deep breath. If we're in an accident, that's only going to slow us down from getting to her."

"Dad, my baby is in surgery."

"I know, honey, but I can't drive, so you have to keep it together."

Brooke brushed her tears away, took a deep breath, and began to count the mile markers. She put her emergency flashers on, gripped the steering wheel tightly, and pressed the gas pedal. Nothing was going to stop her from reaching Olivia.

~

Brooke ran into the hospital, leaving her father to follow her slowly. He'd told her to go on and that he'd catch up to her.

Amelia met her at the hospital door.

"She's still in surgery," Amelia said. "They're doing a splenectomy now."

Brooke started to cry. "I'm sorry. I should have been here."

"You had no way of knowing this was going to happen."

"Who's operating?"

"Dr. Egbert."

"He's good."

"Yes, he is."

"Brooke, there's something you should know." Amelia paused. "There were some things I had to do. Olivia coded down in the emergency room before they took her up to surgery."

"Oh my God," Brooke said and started to cry again.

The elevator dinged, the door opened, and Brooke stepped into the waiting area. At almost the same time, the doctor came through the doors that led to surgery.

"Brooke," he said. "Glad they found you."

Surprised to see Colin standing against the wall, she watched as he pushed off and joined her and the doctor.

"Doctor," he said.

"How's my baby?" she asked.

"Olivia is doing much better, now. She's still under the anesthesia and will be for a while. We removed her spleen and evacuated most of the blood from her abdomen. We left a drain in to get the rest. We had to give her two units of blood in surgery to replace what she'd lost. Now we'll just have to monitor her closely for the next twenty-four hours."

"Amelia said she coded down in the emergency room."

"Yes, she lost a lot of blood and went into shock in the ER," he said. "But her heart rate and her pulse are good. Kids are resilient. She's going to be just fine."

"Oh my God, I can't believe I wasn't here," Brooke said.

"Yes, well, Mr. McDermott signed the consent order in your place."

Brooke froze, realization dawning as to what the doctor was saying. She looked at Amelia.

"I'm sorry, I had no choice but to tell him the truth. We needed a signature and you weren't here."

The doctor glanced between the two women.

Brooke took a deep breath. Colin had signed the surgery forms for Olivia. He knew he was her father.

"Thanks, Dr. Egbert. I'm just glad you were able to stop the bleeding and save my daughter."

"When she starts to wake up, they'll move her to a room. I want to keep her here in the hospital for several days."

"Of course," Brooke whispered, a sense of surrealism surrounding her.

The doctor hurried back to the ER.

Brooke faced Colin and stared into the depths of his brown eyes. Her body sagged with relief now that Olivia was okay, but she was not prepared to deal with Colin. But there he stood, his brown eyes colder than a Montana blizzard. The temperature in the room seemed to drop twenty degrees, and Brooke inwardly shuddered.

"We have a child," he said. "Did you ever consider that I might want to know?"

Brooke raised her chin and chose her words deliberately. "She's *my* daughter. Six years ago you said you didn't want children. I took you at your word."

Chapter Six

Close to ten o'clock that night, they wheeled Olivia from the recovery room. Amelia had taken Brooke's father home about an hour ago. Colin had been withdrawn and silent since their initial confrontation in the waiting room.

Brooke followed the stretcher down the hall and into a room. She stood to the side as the nurses moved Olivia from the stretcher and laid her on the hospital bed. She watched as they checked her daughter's vitals, blood pressure, and then the nurses stepped out of the room, leaving them alone. Brooke moved to Olivia's side, waiting for her baby to open her eyes and come back to her. Until Olivia woke up, Brooke couldn't rest.

Colin stood in one corner of the room, watching Brooke, saying little. Until now, they'd not had a moment alone.

Anger radiated from him, hardened his full mouth and smoldered from his brown eyes. How could she blame him? She'd kept her pregnancy from him. She'd been a frightened twenty-one-year-old woman who'd gotten pregnant by accident. She'd gone to tell the father of her child, but before she could get the words out, Colin happened to say he didn't want children. So she'd left. After her final exams, she'd packed her bags and escaped to have her baby.

That way Colin would never know about the baby he didn't want. That way Brooke could keep her baby without the drama of an angry father.

Yet she remembered the night she'd conceived Olivia. After dating for over a month, they had attended his final frat party, where someone had apparently spiked the punch. Dancing and laughing the night away, they'd somehow found themselves in bed together. Sure they'd used protection. But somehow the latex had torn, resulting in

Olivia.

At the time, running from Colin had seemed like the perfect solution. Returning home to parents who loved her and would help her had seemed better than facing a man who never wanted children.

She glanced at her daughter. How would Olivia react once she learned of her father? She'd asked before about her daddy, and Brooke had been purposively vague with her response. Eventually she would have told Olivia the truth, but not until she was old enough to understand. This was the reason she'd put his name on Olivia's birth certificate. If something had happened to Brooke, she wanted Olivia to know the name of her father.

But now…now she would soon learn the truth. Or maybe not.

"Look, I realize you're angry with me," she said, keeping her head down.

"This is why you disappeared without as much as a good-bye?"

"Yes."

"I searched for you!" he said, his voice low and tight as if he restrained himself.

Shocked to learn he'd tried to find her, Brooke turned toward him, her hand resting on her daughter's arm.

"I was stunned when you left."

She sighed, glanced at her daughter and then looked to the angry man standing in the darkened corner. "Colin, you told me you didn't want children."

"I didn't," he said his voice low and fierce. "But I also didn't know you were pregnant."

Brooke checked Olivia for any signs of consciousness. Without looking at Colin, she said, "I tried to make it easy for you. This way you didn't have the responsibility of a child you didn't want."

"Well, thanks for that," he said sarcastically. "Had you

considered that maybe I would have reacted differently if I'd known the situation? Did you ever consider for just a moment that I might have wanted to work something out? Or were you afraid I might have asked you to end the pregnancy?"

She whirled around, her own anger rising. "Why in the hell do you think I ran? Yes, I thought all of those things and knew I had only one option. You're looking at her lying in that bed."

There was a moment of silence in the darkened room as Brooke tried to calm her overwrought nerves. She scanned her baby's face, trying to find some sign she would soon awaken.

"Now we'll never know how I would have reacted to the situation, because you took the decision from me. You ran away with my child," Colin hissed in the darkness.

Exhausted, Brooke ran her hand through her hair. She couldn't take much more tonight. "You didn't want children. I would never have had an abortion. I tried to do what I thought was best for me and Olivia."

Colin glanced at Olivia. "I would never have asked you to have an abortion."

Brooke considered him, his flashing brown eyes, his crossed arms and rigid body. Had she been wrong all those years ago? "But you said no children."

"Yes, I don't know what I would have done. But I would not have asked you to end the pregnancy. Now I have a daughter."

"She doesn't have to know," Brooke said quietly. "We can continue on just like before. She could learn about you when she's older. You could continue on with your life like nothing has changed."

In the darkness, he took two steps toward her. His face was red and his eyes gleamed with anger. "I've just learned I have a daughter. Already you're trying to get me out of the picture. You don't want me in Olivia's life. You don't want me in your life. What are you afraid of?"

Brooke shook her head. "No, you rejected us before she was born. I'm giving you a chance to walk away."

"How could I reject something—someone—I knew nothing about? I'm still trying to adjust to the fact that I'm a father. Could you give me some time before you start kicking me to the curb?"

A groan from the bed drew their attention to Olivia. She stirred, and Brooke grabbed her hand.

"Get a nurse," she told Colin.

He crossed the room in two quick strides and hit the call button.

"Yes," the nurse asked.

"She's waking up," he told the nurse.

"Baby, it's Mom, can you hear me?"

Olivia swallowed and tried to rub her eyes. "Mama?"

"Yes, baby I'm here," Brooke said, trying to hold back the tears.

"I'm thirsty," Olivia said, still not opening her eyes.

The nurse came in the room. She quickly moved to the bed and started to take Olivia's vital signs. "Hey, Ms. Olivia, do you know where you're at?"

"Home?"

"No, sweetie, you're in the hospital," the nurse told her.

Olivia groggily opened her eyes and glanced around. "What happened?"

"There was an accident, Olivia. You were hurt," Brooke told her daughter, holding her hand.

The nurse scanned her forehead for body temperature. "No fever. That's a good sign."

"My tummy hurts," Olivia said, trying to move her hand to her stomach.

"No, baby, it's okay. Don't touch."

The doctor walked through the door. "How she's

doing?"

"She just woke up."

The doctor walked over to the bed. "Olivia, I'm going to check your bandage. Does your tummy hurt?"

"Yes," Olivia whined, still groggy.

The doctor raised the sheet, checked the drainage tube and the bandages. "No sign of bleeding. That's good."

He listened to her heart and checked the heart monitor. "Her pulse has slowed. That's a good thing. Her heart isn't working as hard."

"Olivia, the nurse will give you some medicine and then I need you to go back to sleep. Okay?"

"Can I watch cartoons in the morning?"

"I think we can arrange that."

"Okay. Mommy, will you be here?"

"I'm staying right here beside you. You just go to sleep. I'll be here when you wake up."

"Okay," she said.

The doctor motioned for Brooke to follow him into the hall while the nurse stayed behind, giving Olivia a sip of water. Colin fell into step beside her.

"We need to monitor the drainage tub and make sure there's no swelling in the abdomen for the next twenty-four hours, but right now it appears that the worst is over, barring no infection. I think she's going to be all right."

Brooke sighed with relief, feeling as though she would crumple to the floor.

Colin automatically reached out and steadied her in his arms. She started to cry and wrapped her arms around his neck, holding onto him.

"Hey, I gave you good news," the doctor said.

"I'm so relieved."

"Brooke, try to get some rest. She'll need you the next few days," the doctor said, patting her on the back.

"Thanks, doctor."

Colin continued to hold her while she cried. Finally, she pulled out of his arms.

"I'm sorry," she said. What was she doing, leaning on Colin when there was so much anger radiating from him?

"It's okay," he said gruffly. "It's been a tough day."

"Yes," Brooke said wiping her eyes. "It's okay if you want to leave now. You don't have to stay. I'll be here."

Colin clenched his fists.

"Don't think that just because I comforted you through your crying jag that we're finished discussing Olivia. I'm leaving, but we're not through with this discussion," he said, his voice rough.

Brooke glanced at him through tear-spiked eyelashes. "You don't want her. You saved her life, and I'm appreciative, but you've done your part. You can leave."

Colin took a deep breath and ran a hand through his hair. "Not so fast. I don't know what I want, but just because I'm not jumping right into the daddy role doesn't mean I don't want it, or her. And don't think I won't take care of her. She will have my protection."

"What do you mean 'protection'?"

"No child of mine will lead the life I had, living in and out of homeless shelters. I will pay my part of her support. You will take good care of my daughter," he said walking away from Brooke.

Brooke watched his retreating back, confusion spreading. What was he talking about? He'd lived in homeless shelters?

~

Colin walked out of the hospital toward his car, the cold, night air slapping him in the face, causing him to huddle in his coat. He had a daughter. A five-year-old little girl. Even before he'd known she was his, he'd liked her. And now he'd learned she was his flesh and blood.

From one broken condom, he and Brooke had created this child with a mischievous smile and brilliant green eyes like her mother's.

Why hadn't Brooke confided in him all those years ago? Why hadn't she told him the truth? No, children hadn't been in his plans, but he hadn't realized at the time that she was pregnant. It'd never crossed his mind that one encounter, and they'd created a baby.

He reached his car, opened the door, and sank into the driver's seat.

What should he do? His mother had been a single mom. They'd lived in and out of homeless shelters. When the work dried up, they were evicted. Then they lived on the streets or in a shelter until she found another job.

For the first seven years of his life, all he remembered was being afraid to get too comfortable in any apartment—they'd be moving soon. And the hunger. God, he remembered going to bed at night his belly aching for food. At least in the shelter, there was always something to eat.

As an adult he'd realized how lucky he'd been when his mother finally dropped him off at his grandmother's. Still, to this day the loss of his mother hurt, leaving an empty void in his life. After she left, every time the phone rang, he hoped it would be her.

Then one day he just stopped caring.

He'd sworn that he'd never have children and risk them growing up hungry and cold. But now he had a daughter. It still stunned him. Though Brooke seemed like a good mom, he wondered if Olivia had ever been hungry. Or cold? Or without shelter?

He hit the steering wheel with his fist, anger spilling from him.

What did he do? Drive away, never look back and just hope that Brooke took good care of Olivia? Send child support every month so that his child received the care she needed but be an absentee father?

A child needed both parents. Hadn't he always yearned for his mother and father? Yearned to have a normal life like other kids?

What a crappy way to find out he was a father. What a crappy thing Brooke had done to him and their child.

Now he had to decide, did he become involved in Olivia's life or simply disappear?

His mother had walked away and left him behind.

What would he do?

~

Around eight o'clock the next morning, Brooke glanced up as Amelia strolled into the room. Olivia was awake, watching her cartoons.

"Hey, Olivia," she called.

"Hi, Amelia," Olivia said sleepily.

The cartoons were on, but she slept through most of them, the pain medication keeping her drowsy.

"Do you mind if I steal your mom away for a few minutes? I'm going to take her to the cafeteria and insist that she eat something."

"Sure," Olivia said, her eyelids drowsy.

"Are you sure, honey?" Brooke asked.

"Go, Mom," she said. "Just come back fast."

Amelia laughed. "Bright kid."

Brooke followed her friend down the hall.

"Thanks, I needed a break."

"You've been here all night. You need to go home and get some real sleep."

"Maybe later," Brooke admitted.

"How's she doing?"

"Good. If she continues doing well, they'll remove the tube later this afternoon. They may release her tomorrow."

"Great!"

Reaching the cafeteria, they filled their plates with eggs and snagged two steaming mugs of coffee. They found a table, and sank onto chairs.

Starving, Brooke savored the bite of scrambled eggs. She'd missed supper last evening and hadn't left Olivia's side all night. Her father had promised to come up and relieve her this afternoon. She intended to take him up on that offer. A quick shower, a little nap, and she'd be back.

So far Colin had yet to return. She hoped he never returned. Though her mind screamed *liar*. She wanted to see him again.

"So did Colin ever say anything else last night?"

Brooke sighed. "Yes, after everyone left, while we were waiting for Olivia to wake up, he finally spoke up."

"And?"

"I don't know. He left here angry, but I don't know if he will return and be her father or disappear again."

Amelia's blue eyes beseeched her. "I hope you understand that I felt I had no choice but to tell him the truth. I can't help but think if I hadn't known, the outcome could have been so different."

"I know I didn't appear very grateful last night, but at the time, I didn't understand the severity of the situation. Thank God you told him," Brooke said. "If he hadn't been here…" She shuddered. "I can't think about that. I just can't."

"Look, I'm sure you had your reasons for keeping the truth from Colin. I don't know much about the man except that he plays a good Santa," she said, smiling.

"Don't think too highly of him," Brooke said, shaking her head. "He told me he never wanted children. When I found out I was pregnant, I skipped town."

Amelia stared at Brooke in disbelief. "How old was he? Men say stupid things all the time. Maybe he's grown up now."

"Or he still might not want my daughter."

"Then I'd think he was just an asshole, and it would be in her best interest not to know her father." Amelia leaned back in her chair.

Brooke laughed. "That's what I like about you. You're always brutally honest with me."

"Yeah, it keeps the men away," she said.

Amelia gave Brooke a look over the top of her coffee. "What's it like seeing Colin again? Are there any embers still burning from college?"

It was a question that Brooke had asked herself over and over. But she didn't know the answer. The last twenty-four hours had been too stressful. There had been no time to consider how the news of Olivia's parentage would affect Colin or whether she truly wanted him in their lives. They didn't need him. Before he'd returned, she'd fantasized about him learning of Olivia and the three of them creating a family. But that was a single mother's fantasy, not reality.

If given the chance, would she want him permanently in their lives?

"To be honest, I haven't had time to think about the implications of Colin learning about Olivia. If he comes around, he'll tell us what his intentions are. Or we could never see him again. I just don't know."

"So you feel nothing."

The memory of Colin holding her last night when the doctor had finally said that Olivia was going to be okay returned, and she remembered the feel of strength in his arms. A sense of coming home and support had overcome her, and she'd resisted those feelings.

Last night didn't count. They'd both been under tremendous stress as they watched Olivia fight for her life. Emotions had been pinging faster than a computer. If he returned, their next meeting could be quite interesting.

"Right now I'm numb from worry and lack of sleep. Ask me that question again later, when I've had some rest and my daughter is home recovering."

~

Her father came into the hospital room carrying a stuffed teddy bear and balloons.

Brooke rose to greet him, putting her finger to her lips. "She's asleep right now."

He sat the teddy bear in a chair and put the balloons where Olivia would see them when she woke.

Brooke took her father's hand and led him out into the hall. When they stepped through the door, he gave her a hug.

"How's she doing?"

A phone rang at the nurse's station, and people walked down the hall, looking for relatives' rooms. Brooke felt as if she'd entered another dimension of the hospital, one she'd never seen, the family side.

"She's doing better," Brooke said, her voice cracking.

He put his arms around her and hugged Brooke again. "What's the doctor said?"

"If she continues doing well, they may remove the drain later today. They just want to make sure that no infection sets in before they send her home."

"That was a close call for our girl," he said. He released Brooke, but continued to watch her.

Brooke swallowed and laid her hand on her father's arm. "So what do you think of Colin?"

"It was obvious last night that he was angry. No man likes to learn he has a child in the middle of an emergency situation."

"Yeah, he's not very happy with me right now."

"Did you get a chance to talk last night?"

"A little," she said.

"What happens now?" he asked.

"I don't know. I'm hoping he will just go away," Brooke said, not willing to listen to the voice that again called her a liar. "But Colin said something strange last night."

"What?" her father asked.

"He said he'd pay his child support. That no child of his would live the kind of life he had, in and out of homeless shelters."

Her father frowned and shook his head. "That doesn't sound like a man who isn't going to be a part of his child's life. That sounds more like a man determined to make certain his child has a home and food on the table."

The paging system in the hospital came on, and they waited for the announcement to end.

"I've been sitting here thinking about this all morning. I'm really nervous."

"You've had Olivia all to yourself for the last five years. Are you ready to share her?"

Brooke cringed inside. Olivia was her daughter. *Her baby,* and she refused to share her with anyone. She'd been the lone parent from the day Olivia had been born. There'd been no relief from the midnight feedings, the stinky diapers, or a colicky baby. Somehow she'd taken care of her alone. "No."

"You may have no choice. If he's her legal father, he has rights to see his daughter. A judge will make certain of that."

"I wish he would just disappear and never come back," Brooke said aloud, but deep inside that voice of reason and truth whispered *liar.* She didn't need complications with Olivia, yet Colin could still ignite a flame. Hidden beneath her mommy persona was a woman who still found Colin attractive. Even deeper was the woman who would like a second chance with him.

But Colin hadn't acted like he wanted her and Olivia.

He'd sat in his apartment six years ago and spoken of how he didn't want children. Now was a little late to change his mind.

Brooke peeked in the door to see if Olivia had awakened yet.

"What do I tell her, Dad? Do I tell Olivia she has a father?"

"Well that depends," he said. "I think I'd wait and let Colin's actions show me if he's decided to take part in her parenting. There's no sense in upsetting Olivia if the guy is just going to disappear."

"That's what I thought, but I'm afraid he's not going to disappear. I'm afraid he's going to insist he be included in her life," she said.

And Brooke would have to face her biggest fear—the possibility of falling for Colin McDermott all over again.

"Let's see what he does before you do anything. He may never come around again, or he may show up later today."

"Yes," Brooke said, her emotions playing tight rope. Part of her hoped he'd gotten in his car and driven out of town and out of their lives while another part of her longed for the strength of his arms wrapped around her again.

What would Colin do? Would he choose them or disappear?

Chapter Seven

Colin sat in his hotel room, looking out the window at the falling snow creating a winter wonderland that reminded him of all the reasons he hated Christmas. He gripped the phone, listening as it rang four times. Finally, his grandmother answered.

"Hello," she said.

"Hi, Grandma," Colin answered. It'd been way too long since his last phone call.

"Colin, it's so good to hear your voice. I've tried to call you, but I know you're busy."

"Sorry, Grandma. I'm in a contest to win the western sales director position. I've been working sixty hours a week. Are you alright?" he asked.

She laughed. "I'm still standing, and that's saying a lot for an eighty-five-year-old woman. I'm okay. I try to stay involved with the seniors here at the home. I've become a mean bingo player. How about you, Colin? What's going on in your life besides work?"

He cleared his throat as the emotions rushed up in him clogging his windpipe and keeping him from answering. He wanted to ask her about his mother. In the years since he realized his mother wasn't returning, they'd stopped talking about her. He needed some answers, but didn't know how to ask the questions.

"I saw my old girlfriend from college," he said, wondering where to begin, hating how Brooke had kept secrets from him. "Good. How's she doing?"

He longed to confide in her about Olivia, but he wasn't sure he'd choose to see her again. What if he followed the family precedent and walked away?

"She's good."

"Is she married?"

"No," he said.

"Why don't you ask her out on a date?"

Dating? Oh, that was not even a question at this time. With everything that lay between them, Brooke still managed to make his heart race and his body tighten at the sight of her. But how could they even consider dating? Though he still felt captivated by Brooke, and when he'd held her in his arms last night…it seemed right. Yet, part of him hated her for keeping the news of his child a secret.

"No, that's not a good idea," he said.

"Are you okay?" she asked. "You sound stressed."

He laughed. If only she knew. "Yes, work is getting to me."

"You work way too hard, Colin. You've got to stop and enjoy life. You need to find a woman who will be your friend and companion. My time is limited," she said softly. "I don't want you to be alone."

A lump filled his throat, and he had to swallow to keep the tears at bay. "I know, Grandma. And I can't imagine my life without you. You're the only family I have."

The line went silent for a moment. "When are you going to come see me?"

How did he answer that question? If he won the western division sales position, he would have to leave immediately for California. There would be no time for the holidays or any good-byes. He would board a plane and head for the west coast. Somewhere between now and the winning announcement, he had to visit her.

"Soon, Grandma, very soon," he promised.

There was silence again.

Finally, she asked, "If you win this promotion, will you have to move?"

He hadn't intended to tell her until he won. If he was going to earn a million dollars, he needed this position.

"I'll move to Los Angeles."

"Oh," she said.

"I'll return every few months for sales meetings. Our headquarters are still in Denver."

She didn't say anything, and he knew he'd made her sad.

"I gotta go, Grandma. I wanted to check on you and make sure you're all right."

"I'm fine. I'll see you soon. Bye, Colin."

"Bye, Grandma," he said and hung up the phone.

He'd called her to ask her about his mother and once again been unable to talk about her. Years had passed since they'd spoken of her. Not since he was a kid. But learning of Olivia had brought back memories of his mother and made him wonder about his father. Who was his father?

Had his mother ever contacted his grandmother? He needed to know if she knew what happened to his mother. He needed to understand his past so he didn't repeat the same mistakes his mother had. But how could he find out if he couldn't bring himself to say her name.

Colin held the phone in his hand. What did he do? His grandmother had raised him. She'd made certain he'd had food on the table and clothes to wear. She'd taken him to school and helped him with his homework. Because of her, he'd gone to college.

From the day he'd arrived at her home, she had become the stabilizing adult in his life. He'd already missed the first five years of his daughter's life. Did he commit the same cowardly act his mother had and walk out of his daughter's life never to return? Or did he step up to the plate like his grandmother?

No, he hadn't wanted children. The responsibility scared him. What if he and Brooke were killed in an accident tomorrow? Who would take care of Olivia?

He had his grandmother, but who would take care of his daughter? Or would she find herself in foster care, abandoned just like he'd almost been? He'd never been in foster care, but only because his grandmother became his guardian.

Olivia's bright green eyes and sweet smile swam before him, and he clenched his fists.

There really was no decision. He knew what he had to do. He found his attorney's name in his contact list and pushed the call button.

~

Alone in the darkened hospital room, Brooke watched her daughter sleeping. In an hour she would awaken and be bored. Olivia already wanted to get out of bed and go down the hall to the playroom on this floor.

Brooke flipped through her magazine, her eyes registering the ads, but her mind replaying over and over her last conversation with Colin. Had she been wrong not to tell him about Olivia?

Why had she never thought to ask him why he hadn't wanted children? Was there a specific reason? A health issue, something in his history or some other problem that made him decide never to have kids?

The phone rang, and she grabbed it on the first ring to keep from waking Olivia from her afternoon nap.

"Brooke, Colin McDermott asks that you join him in the conference room across from the nurse's station," the nurse told her.

Her heart skipped a beat, and she knew the time of reckoning had come.

She glanced at Olivia sleeping peacefully. She hated to leave her alone. "Thanks. Would you please check on Olivia? She's sleeping right now."

"I'll check on her every few minutes and come get you if she wakes."

"Thanks," she said and hung up the phone.

Rising from the chair, she peeked at her daughter one

last time. Her feet seemed filled with lead as she walked out of Olivia's room and down the hall toward the conference room.

At the time of the pregnancy, she'd made the best decision she could. There was no going back, no changing anything. They would have to move forward.

Brooke stiffened her spine, held her head up, took a deep breath, and stepped into the conference room.

Colin stood by the window, staring at the street below. He turned toward her when she walked into the room. "How's Olivia?"

"She's sleeping right now, but she's doing much better," Brooke said. Tension held her hostage as she unclenched her fists. The memory of the two of them together in college surprised her. His looks had only improved with time. Today, he stood frowning at her, the sunlight bathing his face, and she remembered why she'd been enamored of him.

He sighed. "Good. Have a seat."

Brooke sat down, and he sat across from her.

He folded his hands on the table and gazed into her eyes. "By speaking to you, I'm going against the advice of my attorney."

"You've spoken to an attorney?" she asked, stunned. She folded her hands on top of the table. "Why?"

"He didn't want me to talk to you, but rather have us meet in court. I'd like to try to work things out without a judge," he said, his eyes cold.

"Okay, but what do we have to work out? Olivia is my child. If you think you're going to take her away from me, I'll fight you every step of the way," she said, meeting him head on, ready to do battle.

"No, I would never do that to her or to you," he said. "Still, she's also my child, and I intend to be in her life."

Part of Brooke felt happy, but fear rocked another part.

He was a single man who had never cared for a child. Was she ready to trust him with her daughter? Was she ready to share Olivia?

"I'm having my attorney draw up papers and setting up monthly child support."

"I don't need your money," she said, trying to keep the defensive edge out of her voice, but knowing she'd failed.

"Maybe not, but my daughter is going receive the care she needs. She will not go hungry."

Shock cascaded through her. "What are you talking about? She's never gone hungry."

"Well, I intend to make certain she's well taken care of. I'm not going to be a deadbeat dad who doesn't provide for his child," he said, defensive.

Brooke took a deep breath, not understanding where this conversation was going. Twice now he'd acted like she couldn't take care of Olivia. Yet somehow she didn't think his comments were directed at her so much as him not wanting Olivia to suffer.

"When you don't know you have a child, you can't be considered a deadbeat Dad."

He ignored her comment. "I also intend to set up a life insurance policy that, if something were to happen to me, she would receive the benefits."

"Okay."

"Do you have a guardianship arranged for her in case something happens to you?" he questioned.

Brooke wanted to reach out and strangle him. "Why all the questions concerning her welfare? Don't you think we should be talking about what your intentions are for her emotionally? I understand that you're going to make certain she's okay financially, though she doesn't need it. What about her emotional needs? Are you going to be a father to her?"

He took a deep breath, and Brooke was certain he would

say no. She felt a moment of disappointment. He still didn't want Olivia or to be a father.

"Yes, I intend to stay in her life. It's important to me that I know she's provided for if something were to happen to me or you."

"Well of course she is. My father has legal guardianship, or my sister, if my father isn't alive," Brooke said. Didn't he realize Olivia's welfare had been her concern since the day she'd arrived? Or did he think she couldn't care for her daughter?

"Don't you think I can take care of her?" she asked.

He shook his head. "No. I just need to make certain she has a guardian if something were to happen to either one of us."

Brooke watched him and realized he was scared. There was more to his concerns that he wasn't telling her. She could feel it and see the worry in his eyes. But why, and what did that mean for Olivia?

"How do you intend to be in her life? You're not going to be here for a few days, make a big splashy announcement, and then disappear. I won't have my daughter emotionally damaged by you," she said, determined to protect Olivia.

He rolled his eyes. "Come on, Brooke. I'm trying. I really am, but I don't know much about kids. Give me a break! I don't know how to be a father. It's not as if I grew into the role. I got forced into this."

Brooke felt her nerves stretch into next week, and her ire reached the limit of her tolerance.

"Wait just a damn minute, buddy, no one is forcing you to do anything. You can walk out that door right now and never see us again, and that'd be fine." She leaned back from the table, ready to bolt for the door.

"But that's not going to happen. I used the wrong word. I don't mean forced. I have to learn how to be a father," he said, his brown eyes beseeching her. "I never had a father, so I don't know what's expected of me. I'm sure you were one of those women who automatically became a mother the day she was born."

He didn't have a father? Where had his father been? It dawned on her that he'd never spoken of his father. For that matter, he'd never said much about his mother. She vaguely remembered him mentioning his grandmother.

Brooke thought back to the days when Olivia first arrived. The knowledge she was responsible for that tiny baby had terrified her. She'd feared that she would somehow hurt or damage her forever, but she'd also fiercely loved and protected her.

"No, the first few weeks were hell. I didn't know what I was doing. I worried I would hurt her somehow. I had to grow into the role," she admitted.

"Then give me a little patience. I'm doing the things I know how to do, but I have no idea how to be a father."

"So you contacted an attorney. What do you want?"

He shrugged. "Time to get to know my daughter. I'd like to tell her I'm her father. Watch her grow up. Be a part of her life."

"Why?" Brooke asked. "You didn't want children. I gave you the opportunity to walk out that door and never return. Why the sudden change of heart?"

"I didn't know you were pregnant, or I might have felt differently."

"No, you were pretty adamant that day. You didn't want children."

"Give me a break. I was young, and without getting into all the details, I didn't have the easiest childhood. In fact, the first seven years of my life pretty much sucked. I didn't want to risk another child experiencing my childhood. That's why the child support will arrive each and every month. She will have a guardian in case of an accident, and she will never go hungry."

Brooke shook her head. "You keep acting like I'm not taking good care of her. Olivia has everything she needs."

He glared at her. "Poverty is a big issue for single mothers. You're a single mother."

Brooke took a deep breath, trying to relieve her anger. "Okay, you want to be in her life. How do you plan to do that?"

He shrugged. "I don't know. What do kids do? I'm pretty clueless here."

"Why don't we set up times you can come by the house and see her? We can start with maybe once a week and see how that works."

"No, let's start off with three times a week. I may even pick her up after school one day."

"No unsupervised visits until I trust you with my daughter."

He ran his hand over his face, letting his breath out slowly. "You can change that little phrase to our daughter."

Brooke heaved a heavy sigh. "Look, she's not dumb. She's going to pick up real quick that something's different. She's going to ask me why this strange man is coming to visit us. I'm not ready to tell her who you are, because if you suddenly disappear again, she'll be crushed."

"I'm not going to disappear."

"That's what you say now, but when the parenting becomes tough, are you going to be there for her?" Brooke asked, not trusting Colin.

"I'm new to this. I've only known I was a father for the last twenty-four hours, because you didn't tell me you were pregnant!"

Brooke tried to squelch the anger that reverberated through her. She squashed the guilt that followed the hurt feelings. At the time, she'd made the best decision.

"We can argue over that fact for the rest of our lives.

Maybe I was wrong. But you didn't want children, so I ran. What's in the past, I can't change. Now, I'm not going to let you hurt my daughter. So you can forget telling her you're her father until I see that you intend to stay."

~

The nurse knocked on the door and then opened it. "I'm sorry to disturb you, but Olivia is awake."

Colin watched as Brooke stood from the table and hurried out of the room. She seemed relieved to end their conversation. Colin followed her out and down the hall to Olivia's door. She paused before going inside.

"Are you coming in?"

"Of course. I want to see her. We're starting the process of me getting to know her right this moment," he said.

Brooke frowned and pushed open the door. "Hi, baby girl. You're awake."

"Mom, I'm not a baby."

"You'll always be my baby," Brooke said.

Colin could almost see the imaginary line she was drawing in the sand, letting him know that she was Olivia's parent, and would have full guardianship.

Olivia stared at Colin.

"Hi, Olivia. I'm Colin," he said.

"Hi," she responded. "Have I seen you before?"

"You've probably seen me in the hospital. How's your tummy?"

"It's sore. And my mommy won't let me get up out of bed," she said with a pout.

"That must be kind of boring."

"Yeah."

"Do you like to play games?"

"What kind of games?"

"Well, let's see what's in this bag?"

Colin handed over a gift bag, and the child's eyes lit up

in anticipation. She eagerly reached inside and pulled out a Candy Land box and squealed with delight.

He glanced over at Brooke. "I didn't know if she had one or not, but the clerk at the store told me kids her age like to play this game."

"Megan has one of these, and I play it when I go to her house. It's fun! Thank you," she said holding it to her chest.

"You're welcome, Olivia."

The child stopped looking at the game and gave him a quizzical look. "Are you Santa?"

He laughed. "Everyone plays Santa occasionally. Yes, I've played Santa before."

She grinned. "Santa is going to bring me a puppy."

Colin couldn't help but grin and glance over at Brooke, whose green eyes flashed a warning. He didn't respond.

The little girl opened the game. "Look, we can all play. We can spread it out here on the bed, and Mommy, you, and me, can play."

"Oh, I don't think that's a good idea, Olivia. We have to be careful of your tummy. You still have that tube in," Brooke said, shaking her head and glancing at Colin for back up.

"What if we put the board on your hospital tray?" Colin said. "Then we can all play."

"Yeah, put it up there," Olivia said.

Brooke shot him a glare that should have sent him racing for the door, but he only smiled. He wasn't running. Not for any reason, and no glower would send him out the door.

Colin pulled out the instructions and began to read how to play the game.

Brooke took them from him. "It's not rocket science."

He shrugged. "Obviously, you've played before."

"Hasn't every kid played this game?" she said.

"Not me. You'll have to teach me," he said, smiling at

her.

"Draw a card," Brooke said.

Colin drew a yellow card.

"Now move your marker to the closest yellow spot on the board."

Olivia drew a card and moved past him to a red designation on the board. "I went ahead of you. Your turn, Mommy."

Brooke took a card and moved her marker to a green spot between Colin's and Olivia's.

"Mommy, you're between me and Colin." She laughed at Colin. "You're going to lose."

"We just started. Don't count me out yet," he told her and drew a card. "Orange. See, now I'm ahead of you."

She drew the next card, and it was red. She moved her marker right behind Colin. "Here I come. I'm right behind you."

Brooke pulled out a licorice card and lost a turn. Her green eyes rolled.

"Looks like we're leaving you behind," Colin said. "Olivia and I are racing ahead to the finish."

Colin couldn't help but notice the way that Brooke's eyelashes fell on her silky smooth skin. Even with little sleep last night, she looked beautiful.

Olivia tugged on his arm. "Colin, it's your turn."

"Yes, it is." He promptly drew a licorice card, losing his move. "Cra...oh, persnickety doodle."

Brooke snorted. "What did you say?"

He smiled and raised his brows. "Persnickety doodle."

"What does that mean?" Olivia asked.

"It means snotty," he responded.

Brooke frowned at him over the Candy Land board.

"It's not a word for little girls," her mother said.

Olivia giggled at him. "You get in trouble when you say bad words."

"I know."

"It's my turn," Olivia said, and pulled out a card. "Blue."

She moved her piece to the next blue square. "Come on Mommy, now is when you can pass Colin."

Brooke pulled out a card. "Candy cane."

Colin glanced at Brooke and caught her staring at him in a way he hadn't seen a woman notice him in a long time. He liked being with her even though their relationship was tenuous at best. "I have to catch little Miss Olivia before she beats both of us."

Brooke smiled at him. "I'm sure I'll pass you on the next draw.

Colin held his hand over the cards, squeezed his eyes shut and moved his lips.

"What are you doing?" Brooke asked.

"I'm putting my mojo on the cards so I get a good one." Olivia giggled.

Brooke looked at him like she'd never seen him before.

Colin frowned at Olivia. "Don't try this, young lady. This is only for adults."

"What's mojo?" Olivia asked.

Brooke frowned. "Oh, it's a man who acts silly. He thinks he can change the cards with magic."

"But you told me magic isn't real."

"It's not, honey. He's just playing."

Olivia looked at Colin. "You're funny."

He pulled a purple card, which landed him right next to Olivia.

"Oh no, look Mommy, he's about to catch me."

"Well, draw a good card."

Olivia pulled up a blue card that took her into Candy land.

"I won!" she cried.

"You beat me," Colin said.

"We can play again," Olivia said, yawning.

"No," Brooke said just as a knock sounded on the door.

A nurse came in. "Time to take your temperature."

Colin patted Olivia on the arm. "You need to rest and I have to go to work."

"Will you come back to see me?" Olivia asked.

Colin glanced over at Brooke. "Yes, I'll be back soon. You get well."

"Can we play Candy Land when you come back?"

"We might."

"Okay, see you soon."

"Bye, Olivia."

"I'll walk you out," Brooke said.

She walked him to just outside the door.

"Thank you for trying to make her smile."

Colin frowned. "What did you think I was going to do? Tell her all about the two of us and how I'm her father?"

"I didn't know what your intentions were," Brooke said, her expression tenuous.

"My intentions are to get to know my daughter. And since I've not been around children much, I'm going to need your help."

Brooke nodded. "As long as we're civil to one another in front of her."

Colin shook his head. "I would never argue with you in front of her." Colin leaned in close to her. "You know, we used to have a good time together."

"Now we're different people," Brooke said.

"You may be a clone of Mother Teresa with Olivia, but you're still a woman. A very attractive woman, and I'm still a man. We're going to be spending a lot of time together. Why not at least be friends?"

Brooke licked her lips and cocked her head, her expression bewildered. "You're the one who's been angry. She's my daughter."

"Oh come on, you've been angry too. You told me I could leave," he said.

"You're right. We've both been angry," Brooke said her expression bewildered.

Colin paused and tried again to use his best salesman pitch. "Since we have a daughter in common, it would be a lot easier if we got along. We still have a lot to work out, but can we do this without fighting one another? What's in the past, we can't change, but for Olivia's sake, can't we be friends?"

She bit her lip, her emerald eyes hooded. "Okay, let's try to be friends…for Olivia's sake."

Chapter Eight

Gabriella shimmered into view beside Devon as he stood watching Colin walk out of the hospital. "It's not looking so great for you, hot shot. I'd say that Colin learning that Olivia is his daughter turned out to be a good thing."

Devon faced Gabriella. She watched his eyes widen in shock. "How do you get away with these outfits?"

"What, this?" she asked, gazing down at the short, white leather skirt and white boots. "I'm attending a convention where a lot of ladies of the evening are working. I'm trying to save a sixteen-year-old girl from joining the oldest profession. If I appear in white robes, do you think she's going to listen to me?"

"You get the best cases."

She couldn't restrain her grin. "Yes, the creator does take good care of me."

Together they watched Colin walk to his car.

"So are you ready to give up?"

"Not even a consideration. Colin hasn't begun to deal with parenting yet. And Brooke he's still angry with her, yet fighting the attraction he can't ignore."

Gabriella smiled. "Yes, isn't it wonderful? I'm so happy they're being forced to work together to solve their problems."

Devon shook his head. "No, I intend to tear them apart. Money is his center, and he wants that million dollars more than anything. More than he wants Brooke and Olivia."

"Colin needs the security the money offers. And he can still have a goal to make a million dollars, but when he learns to forgive his mother, that's when he'll find the path to happiness." Gabriella faced Devon. "He's taken the first step by telling Brooke he plans to be a father to Olivia and asking for her help. Your little plan backfired. Actually you made my job easier. Thanks, Devon!"

Devon growled. "It's not over yet. Colin has a lot more to face than just the fact that he has a daughter. Don't start acting cocky yet."

"An angel act cocky? I don't think so." She glanced down at her outfit. "Though we do get to play a lot of roles where no one suspects who we are. It's a great job."

Devon shook his head at her. "You are such a pain in the ass to work with."

She smiled. "Only when you hurt innocent bystanders and small children. Then I put the white boxing gloves on, more determined than ever to save Colin from you. Game on, Devon. Game on."

Gabriella disappeared before he could respond.

~

Colin's cell phone rang. He glanced down at the screen and recognized his boss's number. He hit the Bluetooth button on his steering wheel. "Colin McDermott here, the new western sales director."

Ed laughed. "I like your confidence, Colin. I really do. I haven't heard from you in several days. How's it going?"

"The sales meeting was quite a shocker, Ed."

"Yeah, I know. I couldn't say anything in advance. Logan brought in that sale at the last minute." Ed took a deep breath. "How are you? Any new sales to report?"

"Right now I'm heading to a new prospect in town, plus I'm waiting on decisions from two others. Next week my schedule is to go to Montana and hit the hospitals there."

"Good to know. I was beginning to get worried about you since I hadn't heard from you. I didn't have any new sales reports."

"That's because I've been working."

"Logan had an interesting photo of you. Santa?"

Colin resisted the urge to curse. "All in the name of a

sale, sir. The hospital board smiles upon vendors who donate time to their hospital. That suit will probably get me my biggest sale of the season."

Ed laughed. "I knew there had to be more to that picture than what Logan said. He told everyone you were so certain of winning that you took time off to play Santa."

Jerk, Colin thought.

"You know how bad I want this position. This past year I've worked very hard to earn that spot. If someone told me running through their hospital naked would get me a sale, you know I'd strip down and take off," Colin replied, turning into the hospital parking lot for his appointment.

Ed chuckled. "You are definitely committed, Colin.

Yet for the last seventy-two hours, Colin knew he hadn't been focused on his job like before. Finding out he had a kid in the emergency room sort of took his attention away from the job. Time was short, and he had to concentrate on the goal.

"Has Logan turned in any sales?"

"Not yet."

"Good. I hope to finalize one this week."

Ed paused for a moment. "Are you certain about this move to California? I know your Grandmother is getting on in years. I plan on retiring in the next few years. You could always wait and take my position."

Colin thought about it for a moment. "Thanks, Ed. I appreciate the offer, but I've been working toward this goal all year. I'm not losing it now."

"Okay, but I wanted to throw out that offer to you. You've always been my number one salesman."

"Tell your secretary to get ready to book my flight to California," Colin said, though suddenly he remembered Olivia and Brooke. Somehow he would handle the situation from California.

Ed laughed. "Always so self-assured. I like that about

you, Colin."

Colin disconnected the Bluetooth. Self-assured? He could fake it better than anyone. He'd learned to hide fear and pain a long time ago. Being the best salesman at his company kept money in his pocket and the hunger monster at bay. Never again would he experience that gnawing pain.

Yet he no longer had that cocky certainty that he would make his goal. His focus had been on Brooke and Olivia, not the next big sale.

By now he should have had at least one sale and two-three more sitting in the background percolating. If he let his prospects folder dry up, then his sales were going to dry up. A terrific salesman always had twice as many prospects as he thought he needed.

For the first time since he'd started this job, his personal life had interfered. Brooke's image filled his mind, suddenly leaving him confused. Seeing her again had been startling. Learning they had a daughter together had upended his world.

The college drama of calling her over and over again, of going to her apartment and no one being there, had rattled him that final year. Now he knew why. And while part of him resisted forgiving her for not telling him about the pregnancy, the other part remembered that conversation well. He'd been adamant about his decision never to have children. Yet he hadn't known she was pregnant.

Why had he never tied that conversation to the reason she disappeared? Why had he never considered the possibility she was pregnant? After all, the condom had broken that night and they'd laughed about it, reassuring one another. What were the odds she'd get pregnant?

Obviously pretty darn good.

Why, in the most pivotal days of his career, had the universe dropped Brooke back into his life?

Now here he was six years later with a daughter and the woman he'd always remembered. Out of all his old girlfriends, she was the only one he would like a second chance with.

He'd like to take the relationship out for a test drive. See if that connection they felt was still the same or even better. But would Brooke be willing to let him close? Because no matter what happened between the two of them, he still intended to be a father to Olivia.

~

Later that evening Colin walked down the hospital corridor on his way to see Brooke and Olivia. He carried a gift bag filled with a LeapPad. He didn't know if she had one, but it was the latest gadget to help children learn to read—or so the toy store attendant had told him.

Since Olivia was still confined to bed, he thought keeping her occupied was the least he could do. And it might be educational too. His grandmother had instilled in him from the moment he went to live with her the importance of education and how learning was the way out of poverty. He'd experienced enough poverty to last him a lifetime. So he needed to help Olivia realize the importance of becoming an exceptional student.

As Colin reached her hospital door he noticed a gray-haired man standing outside. He recognized Brooke's father from the night of the accident. That night they had not spoken.

"Hi, Colin," he said. "There was a lot of tension night before last, and I was out of it from my dental work, so we never were properly introduced." The elderly gentleman held out his hand. "Frank Warren, Brooke's father."

Colin shook his hand. "Good to meet you, sir."

"Can I buy you a cup of coffee?" he asked. "They're bathing Olivia, so we can't go in right now."

"Sure," Colin answered, wondering what Brooke had told her father of their situation.

The two men walked down the hall and took the next elevator to the cafeteria. Once they had their coffee, they found a table.

For a moment, they sat across from one another, each man checking the other one out. This man would be his daughter's guardian if something happened to him and Brooke. This man would raise his daughter, like his grandmother had taken care of him.

The cafeteria workers were busy wiping down the tables and closing everything except the vending machines for the night.

"Brooke tells me you played Santa for the kids a week ago."

Had it already been over a week since he played Santa? Time was flying. The contest would soon end, and he had yet to make a sale.

Pressure mounted every time he thought about his work.

"Yes, they needed someone to play Santa. I was here trying to make a sale, and Amelia asked me to fill in. Since then I've done it once more, and they need me again next week."

"Did you enjoy it?"

"Yes and no. The suit is hot, and well, some of the kids can be brats, but then some of them are so excited. It's impossible not to enjoy being with them. I've never been around kids much."

"No brothers and sisters?"

"Nope, it was just me and my grandmother."

"Oh," Frank said. His brows drew together in a frown, and he took a deep breath. "I know things are tense between you and my daughter, but I wanted to tell you, thanks for making certain that Olivia received the surgery she needed."

Colin frowned. "She's my daughter. I would have done anything to save her. And the reason things are tense is because I didn't know about Olivia until that day."

Frank smiled. "I understand. I hope you and Brooke can come to some kind of arrangement that works for all of you, but especially Olivia. My granddaughter is a pretty special little girl."

"And I'd like to get to know my daughter," Colin said.

"Do you plan on telling Olivia you're her father?"

"I'd let her know tomorrow, but Brooke wants to wait. She's afraid I won't stick around."

Frank smiled at Colin. "One thing you have to understand about my daughter, she's always taken great care of Olivia. She's a fierce mama bear that protects her cub."

"I'm glad to hear that, but Olivia is my daughter, too. And I'm not going anywhere."

Yet, if he won the position, he would leave for California. His heart squeezed at the thought, surprising him.

"Give Brooke some time, and she may learn to trust you. Then the two of you can sit down together and explain everything to Olivia."

"I'll wait for a while, but not long."

"Good. Tell me about you and my daughter."

Colin smiled. "We met in college. Everything was fine until she disappeared. I know we have lots of things to overcome—me telling her that I didn't want children and her not telling me about the baby. I can't help but wonder what we would have done about Olivia if she'd told me."

Frank leaned back in his chair and nodded to Colin. "Her mother and I tried to convince her to call you, but she refused. Now that I've met you, I also wonder what you would have done."

"There are reasons I didn't want children. Things I still need to work out, but Olivia is a pretty neat kid. I wish I'd known her sooner."

Colin paused a moment, stunned at the realization that he'd just experienced. What was happening to him? He wouldn't have chosen to have children, and yet now he was admitting out loud that his daughter was special?

Frank smiled. "Yes, she is, and I don't want her, or my daughter, to get hurt."

Colin smiled. "I understand. Sounds like you watch over them."

"You'll soon understand how a man feels about his child. You're well on the way to being protective of your daughter."

Stunned, Colin sat there realizing the man was right. Already he was developing feelings for Olivia. And feelings for Brooke were simmering below the surface, just waiting for her to invite them up for a spin.

~

Brooke had finished tucking Olivia in when her father and Colin walked into the room together. She glanced at each man, surprised.

"Hi," her father said. "While Olivia bathed, Colin and I went down to the cafeteria and had a cup of coffee."

"Oh," Brooke said. She couldn't help but wonder how the two men had gotten along. They appeared relaxed and at ease with one another.

"Hey, Miss Olivia, how are you this evening?" Colin asked as he walked to his daughter's bedside.

"I want out of this bed," she said with a pout.

"What did the doctor say?" Colin asked Brooke.

"He told her maybe tomorrow. He insisted on one more day of rest. So she's been in bed all day," Brooke said, staring at Colin.

Tonight, in his snug jeans and a polo shirt that clung to his tight abs, she couldn't help but wonder how it would feel to touch him again. His brown eyes were warm like honey as he looked at her, sending a trickle of awareness zipping along her spine.

Abruptly, he turned his attention to Olivia.

"I brought something that might cheer you up," Colin said and handed his daughter the gift bag.

Brooke frowned at him. "You've already given her Candy Land. You didn't need to bring her anything else."

He shrugged. "I'm making up for lost time."

Brooke didn't say anything. It was a subtle reminder of how he'd missed birthdays and Christmases. What could she say with Olivia right there between them?

Brooke glanced at her father, who only raised his brows.

Olivia pulled out the LeapPad learning tablet. "What is it?"

"It's a small computer for kids. You can play games and read books on it. I bought you a couple of games and a book that you can read."

"Will you show me how?"

"Of course."

He pulled it out of the box. "I had the clerk set it up, so all you have to do is switch it on and begin to play."

Brooke moved closer to her father.

"You had coffee with Colin?" she asked quietly.

"Yes, we had a nice chat. I thanked him for saving my granddaughter."

"Oh."

"We also chatted a bit about Olivia."

"And?"

"I like him. Be careful, but try to keep an open mind about Colin."

Brooke frowned. Her father wanted her to consider

Colin? But there were so many unanswered questions between her and the father of her child.

Even with her back to Colin, she was aware of him in the room. Her body prickled with awareness when he walked through the door, leaving her to wonder if what they'd felt for one another in the past was still there.

Yet they would have to overcome one large obstacle. Their past.

Why hadn't she dug further into Colin's reasons for not wanting children when she was young? The shock of him avowing he didn't want children had sent her running, but not now. This time she was an adult, and she needed to know why he'd made those comments. What was in Colin's past to make him say he didn't want children? And why all the questions about Olivia's security?

What about his revelation of being homeless? How old was he when he lived on the streets? Was that the reason for his need to make certain Olivia was cared for?

Colin was bent over the bed, his head next to Olivia's as he showed her how to play a game on the toy he'd bought her. Seeing the two of them together had Brooke's heart stuttering.

High cheekbones, dimpled smile and green eyes, Olivia looked like her father in so many ways. Sometimes she acted like him, too. In the last few days, he'd played the perfect father, visiting his daughter and melting Brooke's defenses.

All the walls she'd thrown up to protect herself were weakening. Once again she could tell she was falling beneath the charming spell Colin created. She longed to believe in him. To have faith that he wanted to be a devoted, loving father to Olivia. To consider him as a man she could give her heart to.

This time, though, she had to think not only of herself, but Olivia. And this time, she wasn't a naïve young college girl, but a woman who knew what she expected from a man.

Was she ready to give Colin a second chance? Or would he only disappoint her again by leaving her and Olivia?

<h1 style="text-align:center">Chapter Nine</h1>

The next day in Olivia's hospital room, Brooke was busy stuffing Olivia's dirty clothes into a suitcase when Colin knocked on the hospital door.

"Hi," he called.

Olivia glanced up. "Colin, I'm going home!"

"Great."

Brooke smiled at him. "Hi. She's a little excited this morning."

"I see that."

"We have to wait until Grandpa gets here. Mommy's car died last night."

Colin frowned at Brooke, "What happened?"

"The battery," she said.

"Where's the car?" he asked.

"It's outside in the parking lot. I went down to bring it around to the front of the hospital, but it won't start."

"Call your dad back and tell him I'm taking you home."

"That's okay, he doesn't mind," Brooke said.

"No, I insist," Colin said. "This way, you can help me find your apartment."

Unease prickled through her. But sooner or later he was going to see their home. He would want to visit Olivia.

She picked up her cell phone and pressed the contact key. "Hey Dad, I don't need that ride any longer. Colin is here. He's going to help me get her home."

She smiled. "Thanks Dad, love you too." She clicked off the phone.

"Do you ever work?"

He laughed. "All the time. I stopped by the hospital to check on the status of the decision regarding the purchase of the RX700 software. Then I have an appointment across town in two hours. While I was here, I thought I'd check on the two of you."

Brooke shook her head at him, but couldn't keep the smile off her face. No matter what, it was a lovely day. Olivia was healing, and as a result, she was taking her daughter home. "One day you show up in this hospital, and now you're here all the time."

He smiled.

"Deal with it," he said, a twinkle in his eyes.

"I don't think a decision has been made on the software yet," she told him, zipping up the suitcase.

"Okay," he said nodding his head. "You'll let me know?"

"Of course."

"Are we ready to go?" he asked.

"I've got her all packed."

"Good," he said.

"Mommy, can we stop and get tacos?"

"No, honey, we need to get you home."

"What if we go through the drive-through and do take out?" Colin asked.

"Yeah," Olivia said, excited. "I'm hungry."

Brooke frowned at the two of them, wondering which one was the adult. At this moment, she would have given her daughter cake if that was what she wanted. "Normally, we don't do fast food, but we'll make an exception today."

"Okay, I'll carry down a load of flowers, while you get Miss Olivia a wheel chair."

"I don't need a wheel chair," Olivia said with a pout.

"Hospital rules say if you're going home, you leave in a wheelchair," Brooke told her daughter. "Do you want to spend a couple more nights here? If so, we can forget the wheelchair."

"I'm going home."

"Then I guess we better find you a wheelchair," she

responded.

Brooke watched Colin hurry out the door, his arms loaded with flowers and balloons. There had been no one to help her, and she hated to depend on her dad. Now Colin was here loading his car.

Why didn't she hate him any longer? Why, whenever she saw him was there this little catch in her throat? Why did her heart beat a little faster? His eyes-good Lord the way he looked at her-had heat zipping along her nerve endings. Right in front of her daughter.

Sure they had so many things to work out yet. Sharing Olivia…she didn't know how to share her daughter. From the time her daughter had been conceived, Olivia had been hers. No one else's.

Yet Colin was Olivia's father.

He came back in the room. "Are we all set?"

"We're ready."

"Your chariot awaits," he said, rolling the wheelchair up to the bed. The nurse's aide helped Olivia into the chair. She pushed her out of the room with Colin and Brooke following.

"Want to race down the hallway?"

Olivia giggled. "Can't. It's against the rules."

"But they won't be able to catch us. We'll race out the door and instead of taking the elevator, we'll use the stairs. I'll give you a push and catch you when you land downstairs."

"You can't catch me. I'll hit the floor," she said, glancing back at Colin from the wheelchair as if were a crazy man.

"Olivia don't believe this silly man," Brooke said, gazing at the child she'd almost lost and counting her blessings that her daughter was healing. Yet watching the two of them together was painful. What had she done?

Colin sighed. "Okay. I guess then we'll have to let the

nurse's aide do her job. It won't be near as much fun, but will probably make your mom happy."

Brooke gave a snort. "When has my happiness been your concern?"

Colin stopped and frowned at Brooke. "Who peed in your Post Toasties this morning?"

Olivia laughed. "She doesn't like Post Toasties. She eats yogurt for breakfast."

"Maybe that's the problem. I bet if she ate some Post Toasties with a little extra fiber, she'd have a bright smile on her face. Instead of getting tacos, maybe we should stop at the store and buy some cereal. After all, it is the breakfast of champions."

"I'm perfectly fine. We're on our way home, and it's a great day." Brooke gave him a warning glance over the top of Olivia's head. "Besides, I thought that was Wheaties?"

"Oh yeah, you're right."

Who was Brooke trying to fool? She wasn't all right. She was a bundle of raw nerves, afraid of making the wrong decision regarding Colin and her daughter. Seeing Colin and Olivia interact was ripping her into shreds on the inside. Colin teased and joked with Olivia and seemed to get along well with her, so why hadn't he wanted children?

God, she so wanted to believe that his remarks that day were those of a young, naïve boy who didn't know what he wanted in life. He was here befriending *her* daughter, and she loved but feared their relationship.

Why had she deprived him of the first five years of his daughter's life if he wanted her? Or was this some big act, and once the newness wore off he'd be gone?

They arrived at Colin's car, and Brooke stared in surprise at the luxury sedan.

"It's my company car," he said with a shrug. "It handles well in snow."

"Oh," she said, trying to keep from laughing. "Let me

get the booster seat out of my car for Olivia."

Brooke hurried off, leaving Colin to finish loading up the flowers and gifts.

When she returned she quickly strapped the child safety seat into the back of Colin's car and bundled Olivia in.

He opened the passenger door for her, and she slid onto the soft leather. The memory of their first date slammed into her consciousness. The way he'd looked so nervous, and how he'd reached out, taking hold of her hand while he drove to the basketball game. He'd been so sweet, so kind, that she'd been smitten almost immediately. And when he'd kissed her goodnight, she'd limped into her college dorm feeling like a hot puddle of wantonness.

"Earth to Brooke," Colin said.

Olivia giggled from the backseat.

"Where do you live?"

"Oh, sorry," she said and gave him her address.

She lived less than ten minutes from the hospital. They went through the local taco drive-through and picked up the family pack.

Brooke tried to pay, but Colin wouldn't let her. Finally, they pulled up in front of her small apartment complex. Snow and slush littered the dead grass, so Colin carried Olivia, since she didn't have her snow boots.

Brooke turned the key in the lock to her front door and held it open for him. "This is our home."

Colin stepped inside and put Olivia down. "You're almost too big for me to carry."

"I'll be six next month. That's a big girl."

"Yes, it is," he said, his voice distracted.

Brooke watched him glance around the apartment and take in the living area off the kitchen and the two bedrooms at the back of the apartment with a connecting bathroom.

"Why don't you carry the tacos to the table while I help Colin bring in your stuff?" Brooke said to Olivia.

"No, you stay here with Olivia and I'll bring everything in," he insisted.

Again, it felt good to have a helpmate, someone who took care of her for a change. Yet she couldn't become too accustomed to his help.

Brooke and Olivia set the table while Colin brought in the flowers and gifts Olivia had received.

Finally they all sat down to eat. As they ate their tacos, Olivia kept glancing between Colin and Brooke. She could almost see the questions forming in her daughter's mind.

"Colin, do you work with my mom?"

"No, I knew her years ago."

Brooke glanced at Colin. "We went to the same college."

"Did you know my daddy?" she asked Colin. "He went to school with my mommy."

Brooke almost choked on her taco. Her eyes pleaded with Colin not to tell Olivia the truth.

Colin glanced at her, his darkened eyes speaking volumes to Brooke as he finished chewing and wiped his mouth. He was going to tell her. She could feel it in her bones. He was going to go against her wishes and tell Olivia he was her father.

"Yeah, I knew him. He's a great guy. Worked real hard, and finished his degree. Someday he'll be a millionaire. He would want you to do well in school."

"Mom, is that true?" Olivia asked, her green eyes wide and questioning. A frown appeared on her face. "But why doesn't he come see me?"

"Oh, I'm sure he's going to. And very soon, too," Colin said before taking a bite of his taco.

"Mom, did you hear that? I'm going to meet my daddy."

Brooke was trying to swallow the taco that tasted like cardboard stuck in her throat. She glared at Colin. How dare he get Olivia's hopes up. She didn't want her daughter hurt. Olivia would be crushed if he disappeared tomorrow.

"What does he look like?" Olivia asked.

"Well, some women find him extremely handsome."

"And some women are blind," Brooke said.

Olivia glanced between the two of them.

"Finish your tacos, Olivia. You need to get to bed."

Colin ignored Brooke.

"Your father is tall, about six feet. He has brown eyes and dark hair, weighed one hundred and eighty pounds before Christmas. I don't know how much he'll weigh after Christmas," Colin said, his eyes almost daring Brooke to stop him.

"Finish up, Olivia. You need to take a nap," Brooke said, wanting to get Olivia out of the room as quickly as possible.

"Mom, I'm not tired. I've been in bed. I want to talk to Colin."

"Colin has to leave as soon as we finish lunch. He has to go to work."

"Unfortunately your mom is right. I have an appointment in less than an hour, so I have to go," Colin said.

"When will you come see me again?" she asked.

"What if I pick you girls up on Friday night? We can go out to Fred's Christmas Tree Farm and pick out a tree. If you feel like getting out."

"A real one?" Olivia said, her green eyes wide.

"Yes," Colin said, kind of surprised.

"Mom always puts up a fake tree. She says it's cheaper and doesn't make a mess. Plus we aren't cutting down a real tree."

"Olivia, our artificial tree is pretty."

"Yeah, but it would be fun to go pick out a real tree," she said.

"We could go to the tree farm and make an evening of it." Colin said.

"We can bring the tree home and decorate it," Olivia said, her innocent eyes widening with excitement.

Brooke watched the two of them making plans, laughing and talking together. All the questions from Olivia about her father were tearing her up inside. Seeing her daughter so excited to learn her father would come visit her hurt. Had she wasted five years of Olivia's life by keeping her from her father?

And Colin? Good Lord, the man still had the ability to make her crazy. All she think about was the two of them together the night they'd conceived Olivia. The memories returned, slamming her with sensation, leaving her wanting and restless.

And now he was doing things that families did, and she wanted so much to tell him to stop. But she couldn't. For Olivia's sake. She had to play along with this and hope for the best.

"Okay, we can go Friday night if you promise me that you'll rest for the next two days.

Olivia pushed her plate away. "Okay, I'll rest."

Colin stood. "Well, ladies, as much as I hate to leave you, my next appointment awaits."

Brooke stood as well, her plate barely touched. "I'll walk you to the door."

The short stroll held a tense, heavy silence. In the entryway she turned to face him. "Thank you for not telling her. I'm not ready for her to learn the truth yet."

"You'd better get ready, because I'm not going to wait forever," Colin said, standing so close to her she could hardly breathe.

She stepped back, needing the distance to keep a clear head.

"I realize that, but she's had a stressful week with the

accident and almost dying. I don't think now is the time to suddenly say, 'Oh by the way, meet your father'."

"I agree, and that's why I didn't tell her. But I laid the foundation."

"Yes." Brooke wanted to say so much more, but refrained. One step at a time, she told herself. "Look, this is going to be tough for a while. Please give me some time."

"You've already had five years with her. How much more time do you need?"

"That's not fair."

"No, it's not. But it wasn't fair that you kept the knowledge of her from me, either."

"No, it wasn't, but then life often isn't fair."

"Okay. We're at an impasse. I'm trying to play by your rules, but she's my daughter, too." He started to walk out the door, stopped and turned around. "I know we're tree shopping on Friday, but could you get a sitter and plan to spend Saturday with me? I need some help picking out her Christmas gifts."

"I can't."

"Can't, or won't?" he asked. "I thought you could help me find something special to give her."

Brooke stood, thinking, wondering, knowing what her heart wanted while her brain screamed *no*. It would mean being alone with him. Hours together while she tried hard not to let her attraction to him rekindle in any way. But this was for Olivia. The man had no clue what to buy her.

"If you don't go with me, I might be tempted to pick out a puppy."

"Don't you dare," she whispered. "Unless, you have time to take care of the puppy, because there will be no dogs in this apartment."

He grinned at her. "I guess you better go shopping with me."

"All right. We're going shopping, and then we're

coming straight home."

"Okay."

"See you Friday," Brooke said and closed the door as he walked out.

Oh God, she was in so much trouble.

~

Brooke glanced up, as Amelia entered her office and plopped down in the chair across from her. "How's the first day back?"

"Hectic."

"How's Olivia?"

"She's doing much better. Dad's taking care of her the next two days and Saturday."

Amelia raised her brows. "You got a hot date Saturday?"

"No date!" Brooke frowned. "Against my better judgment, I'm going Christmas shopping with Colin."

"Oh. Santa's taking you shopping."

"Yes, he wants to buy Olivia a Christmas present and asked for my help." Brooke sighed.

"Have you told Olivia he's her father?"

"No, I won't let him say anything until I'm certain he's going to stay around. Can you imagine how disappointed and hurt she'd feel if he left and never saw her again?" Brooke said.

She leaned back in her chair and shook her head. Who was she kidding? She was frightened for her daughter and herself. Today's Colin seemed more mature. There was a layer to him that the college student had been missing.

Even with all the issues remaining between them, she liked this Colin better.

"So when are you going to trust him again? How are you going to know? He could walk out the door tomorrow and never come back, or he could wait five years and then disappear," Amelia said.

"I don't know, but I'm not ready to tell Olivia."

Amelia shook her head at her friend. "Wow, girl, your life has been quite a roller coaster ride this week. I'm so thankful that Colin was here."

"Yes, I have you to thank for that."

"Oh yeah, the Santa gig. He's got one more performance," Amelia said with a chuckle. "The kids really like him."

"He wants to hire you for his sales team."

"And give up living the good life here at Crystal Mountain General Hospital? No way. I love schmoozing with the doctors who think I'm too pushy, the nurses who just want me out of their way, and the administration who wishes I'd bring in even more donations. One day I'm going to win the lottery, never to step foot through that door again."

Brooke laughed. "It's not that bad, is it?"

"Oh no? Dr. Van Dross screamed at me to never come into his office again. I'm no longer welcome there, as I always want something."

"Has that ever stopped you?"

"No, but I guess it got to me today. I don't like being pushy, but how else am I going to fund next year's activities?"

"Take a break. Go do something fun with the kids. Once you spend some time with them, you'll have a good time and the desire to help them will return full force," Brooke said. She reached over and squeezed her friend's hand. "It's what you do best."

She shrugged. "Yeah, an outing with the kids always puts things in perspective. What I need is to get laid, but I don't have a date with Santa this weekend."

"You could take my place."

"Nope. I've seen the way he looks at you. He doesn't

stare at me like he's imagining me naked."

"What are you talking about?"

"Oh Brooke, you haven't seen it?" she said, astonished. "Every now and then he looks at you like a cave man about to grab you by the hair, and drag you off to his lair. It's just a flash, but believe me, he's dreaming about doing the nasty with you."

Brooke started to laugh. "No, I haven't noticed that particular look, but if he comes in with a bat in his hand, I'll be wary."

"So, does he have a chance?"

"What do you mean?"

"Does Colin McDermott have a snowball's chance in hell of getting back into your pants?"

Brooke shook her head at her friend and smiled. "Is that really any of your business?"

"No, but I have to live vicariously through you. You're the one who has a man hot on her tail. Me, I'm just a lonely event planner who is surrounded by sick children day and night, and hated by doctors who don't appreciate my fund raising abilities."

"Cut the drama. You do a good job. You've just had a bad day."

"Yeah, I know, but tell me…are you going to give him a second chance?"

"I'm so confused, I honestly can't answer that. The young college kid in me would be back there in a heartbeat. The older mom says wait and let him play his cards. Let him show me if he's truly going to be a father to Olivia or disappear once the job gets tough."

~

"Colin McDermott," Colin said into his cell phone. It was Friday morning, and he was on his way to his last appointment of the week. He now had three hospitals considering his proposals and three more appointments lined up for next week. The position of western sales director would soon be his.

"Hi Colin, Steve Jointer from All Saints Hospital of Montague County. Do you remember pitching us your software last year?"

Colin paused. Calls like this were almost a certain sale. He could hardly contain the excitement in his voice.

"Hi Steve, yes I do. You guys turned me down and went with our competitor."

"Yes, and we've regretted that decision ever since. The board and I are getting together to talk about this tonight over drinks. I was wondering if you could come in, show us your product once again, and give us a bid." Excitement coursed through his veins. This could be the sale that put him over the top. If all of the hospitals purchased, that would be four, including this one. Four in a two week period was outstanding.

But tonight he'd promised Olivia and Brooke they would go tree shopping. The plans were to pick out a tree and then spend the evening decorating it.

Brooke would be furious, but he had to help her understand he had no choice. He needed this sale. They could go Christmas tree shopping on Sunday.

"What time is the meeting?"

"Seven o'clock. We're going to have some dinner brought in, and then we'll adjourn about nine p.m."

Olivia's bedtime.

He couldn't let this opportunity pass by.

"Sure, I'll be there at seven."

"Great. Thanks for doing this on such short notice. I'm sure this is probably going to cut into your personal time."

"Not a problem," he said. "I'll see you tonight."

He immediately dialed Brooke's home number. No answer. He tried her at the office no answer. Crap!

He'd been looking forward to tonight, and he knew that Brooke and Olivia would be disappointed. He tried Brooke's cell phone.

"Hello," she said.

"Hey, it's Colin."

"Hi," she said.

"Uh, something has come up. I'm not going to make tonight."

Silence filled the airways.

"Are you there?"

"Yes."

"Do you want to know where I'll be?"

"Not really."

"You know we're in this big sales push at the end of the year, and if I sell the most I could become the western sales director," Colin said, needing her to understand.

Silence.

"Anyway, I just got a call from a hospital I showed the product to last year. They are meeting with their board tonight. They're not happy with their current software and may switch to ours. I have to be at the meeting and hopefully get the sale."

Silence again.

"Brooke," he said, desperate, not wanting her angry with him. Yet the vibes coming through the phone clearly were not peace and love, or even good luck on the sale. "Tell Olivia, we'll go on Sunday, if you're not busy."

"She got up this morning talking about how today was the day we would pick out our Christmas tree. She's going to be disappointed."

Colin felt his heart clench. How many times had his own mother disappointed him? But he had no choice. He needed this sale.

"I know, and I wouldn't do this except this is a sale I hadn't counted on. This could put me in the win column."

"I knew better than to hope you wouldn't hurt her."

"Hey, I'm not hurting her intentionally. But I have this opportunity. Being with you and her the last few days, I've not made the sales I should have."

"You couldn't say I've promised to spend the evening with my kid, can I get back with you?"

"It doesn't work that way."

"Well it should."

"Look, I feel bad, but I need this sale."

"A sale is certainly more important than your daughter."

"That's not true."

"Good-bye, Colin. Saturday is off as well. I've had a board meeting come up."

Dial tone reached his ears.

Shit! Shit!

Chapter Ten

Early Saturday morning Colin knocked on the door of Brooke's apartment. In his hands he held a bag of donuts and a bag of bagels. An I'm-sorry-please-go-shopping-with-me bribe. He knocked again.

Brooke came to the door in her robe, her eyes heavy-lidded with sleep. "What are you doing here? I told you I had a board meeting today."

"I brought apology donuts and bagels for your board meeting."

She looked down at the bags he held. "You want to feed her pure sugar?"

"Well, I was afraid you'd say that, so I brought some bagels too, as well as orange juice and coffee," he said.

Brooke had never looked more beautiful. Her skin radiated with a morning glow fresh from sleep. The sight of her sleepy eyes triggered the memory of the time they'd studied all night. They'd stopped long enough to drink a cup of coffee and watch the sun peek above the horizon.

"Olivia cried when I told her we weren't going last night. I don't need you upsetting her by making promises you're unable or unwilling to fulfill. She wanted to know if you didn't like her anymore."

"Geez," he said, under his breath. He'd hated to cancel and hoped he could make it up to her. He'd spent the evening torn between the job and Brooke and Olivia. "I'm sorry."

"We don't need you. We were doing just fine before you came into our lives," Brooke said, her eyes flashing with anger.

Colin stood there, guilt eating at him, determined to rectify the disappointment he'd caused his daughter. "That doesn't mean I'm going to stop wanting to see Olivia. She's my daughter," he said softly. "I screwed up. I'll probably screw up again, but I'm committed to Olivia. You're not running me off."

Brooke glared at him. They'd reached an impasse, and Colin feared she would slam the door in his face.

"Who's at the door, Mommy?" Olivia said, the pitter-patter of her feet coming up behind Brooke.

"Go back to the kitchen, Olivia."

"Hi, Colin," Olivia said quietly. "You broke a promise."

Colin knelt down to her level. "I did, and I'm here to apologize. Something important came up at work. I couldn't get out of it. Can I make it up to you by taking you to the farm tomorrow to get the tree?"

Olivia looked up at her mother. "What do you think, Mom?"

"I promise there won't be any other excuses," Colin said.

"Did you get the sale?" Brooke asked.

"Yes, I did," he answered.

"Do you still want to get a real tree, Olivia?" Brooke asked.

"Yes! Oh, yes!"

"Okay, then I'll pick up you and your Mom tomorrow and we'll find a Christmas tree."

"Yeah!" Olivia said, running in circles.

"So can I come in now?" Colin asked.

Brooke sighed, shook her head at him, and opened the door. "Yes, come in."

"What did you bring, Colin?" Olivia asked.

"Delicious things that you can only eat every few months because they'll make you fat."

"Oh..."

"Things your mommy probably doesn't like for you to have."

"Oh, you're being bad," the little girl said with a giggle.

"No, I'm being good," Colin said. "We're having a treat."

"Why don't you guys set the table while I go change," Brooke said and went down the hall toward the bedroom.

"You know being a grown-up means that sometimes our jobs get in the way of our personal lives and what we'd really like to do," he told Olivia as she carried plates to the table and set them out.

"Mommy says her job pays the bills."

"She's right."

"What's your job, Colin?"

"I sell computer programs to hospitals."

"Does mommy's hospital have your program?"

"Not yet."

"You should try to sell it to her. I bet she would like it."

Brooke came back into the kitchen wearing jeans and a sweater. She'd pulled her hair back and put on some makeup. Colin couldn't help but admire the way her hair curled down her back and the soft look of her skin. He wanted to take her into his arms and kiss her, but he knew that wasn't possible.

They sat down to the spread of donuts and bagels. Olivia started popping donut holes in her mouth. "These are really good, Colin. You should be bad more often."

"Not too many of those Olivia. They can make you sick."

"Mm…they're good."

Colin glanced around the small, tidy apartment, aware that the space looked like a home. It appeared Olivia was well taken care of. The living room was full of toys, and there seemed to be plenty to eat. Why he'd doubted that Brooke wouldn't make certain Olivia was provided for, he didn't know. Except his own experience.

When he was Olivia's age, his life with his mother had been the worst. Each time she lost her job, they'd moved from one homeless shelter to another. She'd just gotten a new job when she disappeared for the last time.

He gazed at Brooke. "So has your board meeting been cancelled? Can we possibly go shopping today as planned?"

She shook her head at him. "You make it difficult for me to stay angry at you. Donuts, bagels, and coffee? Works its way around a girl's waistline and sweetens her disposition." She sighed. "Yes, we can go shopping. I've already called my dad, and he agreed to watch Olivia."

"Great. The malls are already open. After we eat, we'll drop Olivia off at your Dad's and away we go."

Olivia frowned. "Why can't I go?"

"Because we're going Christmas shopping. How can we buy your gifts if you're with us?"

"I want a puppy, and I want a Dad."

Silence fell on the table as Brooke and Colin both turned their full attention on Olivia.

"Why do you want a Dad?" Brooke asked, sending an accusatory look at Colin.

Olivia glanced at Colin. "Because I don't have one. All the other kids at school have a daddy."

Colin's chair made a scrapping noise as he stood up from the table and went to refill his coffee at the sink with his back to the table. How could he continue this charade? When was Brooke going to see that they needed to tell Olivia the truth, and soon?

"Parker Jackson at school says that daddies who don't come around don't want their kids."

"Don't believe Parker Jackson," Colin said, whirling around. "I know for a fact that your father wants you."

But he hadn't wanted kids. He was lying. He knew it, and Brooke knew it. They would never know what his reaction would have been to the news that Brooke was pregnant. Probably not acceptable, but now that he'd seen

Olivia, met her and spent time with her, she was a pretty cool kid, and he was proud of the fact that she was his daughter. There was no point in hurting Olivia by telling her the truth—that at the time she was conceived, her father was a dumb-ass.

At that time, he'd been a young college kid who had no idea about the good things in life, only the ones that ripped people's souls out. And his had been ripped out at a very young age.

Colin walked back to the table and sat. He gave Brooke a glance that he hoped she understood. Time was running out.

"Olivia, Parker Jackson doesn't know what he's talking about. Your father can't wait to meet you, and he's sad he hasn't seen you before now."

Olivia nodded "Okay, but like Grandpa says, time's a wastin'."

Colin almost spewed the donut he'd just taken a bite of. The kid had a way with words.

~

"How about this?" Colin said, holding up a baby doll in the middle of the toy store. The place was jammed with people doing their holiday shopping.

"Too babyish. She's getting into the older dolls. I think she's ready for an American Girl."

"What's an American Girl?" he asked.

Brooke laughed. "Just the hottest doll in America. We'll be lucky to find one."

"What else do little girls like?"

Brooke glanced at him. "Didn't you have sisters? Any cousins or females in your house?"

Colin kept walking down the aisle. "It was just me and my grandmother. No one else."

"Oh, I'm sorry."

Colin shrugged. "That's the way life is for some of us. What about you? How are your sisters?"

"You remembered. They're both married," Brooke said, picking up a puzzle and dropping it into the cart. "Is your grandmother still alive?"

"Yes, she's in a nursing home in Denver."

"Do you see her often?" she asked.

"No, but I'd like to take you and Olivia by to meet her. But not until after we tell Olivia I'm her father," Colin said, walking down the aisle and gazing at all the toys with no idea what to purchase for his daughter.

"Stop," she said suddenly. "Look at this. It's Rollerblades."

"She's too young."

"No, she's not. I've lived with her for the last five years. She's ready."

"They're dangerous. Kids get hurt with those."

"I'll teach her."

"How is she going to roller-skate with ten inches of snow on the ground?"

"There are rinks."

Brooke put the skates in the basket. Her eyes dared him to stop her.

"I'm not paying for them," he threatened.

"I didn't ask you to. I've been taking care of her for years without your help."

"Only because you didn't tell me about her."

Brooke's green eyes flashed with anger as she pushed the buggy further down the aisle, leaving him behind.

Colin took a deep breath and released it as he hurried after her. "I'm sorry. We're supposed to be having fun. I screwed up again."

"You do that a lot. No wonder you're still single." She shook her head and glanced at him. "You are still single, right?"

He grinned. "Yes, I've never married."

Brooke picked up several games and tossed them into the cart.

"Why not?"

"Work. It's all I focus on. Sure there have been women, but after they see my work schedule, they don't stick around" he admitted. "What else can I buy her?"

"If you're so busy working to get this promotion that's going to take you out of the state, when are you going to have time for Olivia? How do you think she's going to react when she learns you're her father, but you're moving out of state and never will see her?" Brooke asked, halting the buggy and staring at him.

"I don't know yet. I…I don't know what I'm going to do. I just made the decision to be in her life. I'll work something out," he said, running his hand through his hair.

For several more minutes they continued down the aisle, glancing at the toys. "You can get her that play hair-and-makeup set. Little girls love to imitate their mothers."

Colin tossed it into the buggy. "She's going to be beautiful just like you."

Brooke stopped and smiled at him. "Thank you. That's the first compliment you've given me since you learned I was the evil mother who concealed your daughter's birth from you."

A lady in front of them turned to stare.

Colin laughed as they walked on. "You got her attention."

Brooke shrugged. "Well, it's true. I didn't tell you."

"Are you getting hungry?" Colin asked. "We've been shopping for hours, and the cart is pretty full of gifts. Do you think we could go have dinner someplace?"

Brooke smiled. "As long as you plan on giving me compliments and not calling me the evil mother of your child."

"Only when I'm angry."

~

The mall restaurant was not the romantic hot spot Colin had hoped for, but it was cozy and intimate. Once they were seated, the server brought the wine list, and Colin ordered them a bottle of white.

After the waiter had taken their order and poured the wine, Colin lifted his glass. "To my daughter, a beautiful little girl who looks like her mother."

Brooke smiled and touched the rim of her glass to his. "Thanks."

"Earlier you asked me why I had never married. Why haven't you married, Brooke?" Colin asked.

She smiled. "I've dated. There's been no one that I fell madly in love with or who seemed to love Olivia as I do. I always have to consider her welfare, and whomever I fall in love with has to love her too."

"That's good to hear," Colin said. "After watching and seeing her more, I think Olivia's a very lucky little girl."

"I do the best I can. But it's hard being a single parent."

I've lived that life, he thought to himself. "So when you found out you were pregnant, what did you do?"

"I took my final exams, and then I went home to my family."

Colin ran his hand over his face. "I've thought about that last conversation of ours a lot. I wish I could tell you that I would have been excited about the pregnancy, but I can't. I will tell you that I looked for you everywhere. I tried to find you."

Brooke's eyes widened.

"I even went to the administration office. They would only tell me you were no longer enrolled. That's all. I tried to remember where you were from and only knew it was somewhere in Colorado. I didn't understand why you'd left me."

Brooke reached out and laid her hand on his arm. "I'm sorry. I knew that if I saw you again, I'd break down and tell you about the baby. I feared you would want me to get an abortion. I couldn't do that."

"At that time in my life, I can't say that I wouldn't have considered it. I mean, we were so young, and I didn't want to be a father," he said. He took a deep breath and slowly uncurled his fists.

Brooke stared at him, her green eyes soft and warm in the darkened restaurant. "Can you tell me why you didn't want children? I've often thought I should have asked you why. It could have been for health reasons, and all I did was walk away."

Colin smiled. "My early childhood years were difficult. I never wanted to put a kid through what I went through."

He poured her another class of wine.

"What could be so bad that it would make you never want to have children?"

"Let's just say going hungry as a child is very difficult."

"Oh dear."

"Let's talk of happier times," Colin said, not wanting her to ask him any more questions about his past. He didn't like to talk about the years when he and his mother roamed the city trying to stay warm and dry. "It appears you have it all together. Are you happy?"

Brooke smiled. "Yes, I'm happy. Sometimes it gets lonely, but overall I'm happy. What about you?"

"I like my job, but sometimes I catch myself wondering if there's more."

He reached across the table and picked up her hand. "I want to be successful, independent, and yet you're right, it gets lonely."

She smiled. "Well if you're in line to become the

youngest western sales director, you're doing something right."

"Yes, but what if I wake up one day and discover that I have the prestige of the job, enough money to buy anything I want, and yet I'm still not happy? What happens then?"

"I love my job. But it's not as important as Olivia or my family. After my mother died last year, it reinforced that life is about being with the ones you love." She paused and took another drink of her wine. "So you only have your grandmother?"

"Yes, she's all the family I have."

"What happened to your mom?"

"I don't know."

"What do you mean you don't know?"

"I mean I haven't seen her in twenty years. I don't know where she is."

Brooke's eyes widened in horror, and Colin knew he'd said too much. He didn't want her pity.

"Oh my God. I'm so sorry."

~

Brooke watched Colin carry a sleeping Olivia from the car to her bed in the apartment. She tucked her daughter in and kissed her on the forehead while Colin stood at the door, observing.

She looked at her sleeping child and couldn't imagine never seeing her again. The pain Colin must have suffered as a child, wondering why his mother had left him and never returned. But would that cause him to never want children?

It would definitely make a man want to make certain his children were well taken care of. Now she perfectly understood his questions about Olivia's welfare. But what other damage had Colin's mother done to him?

They tiptoed out of her daughter's room and went into

the living room. Brooke opened another bottle of wine and poured it into glasses. She carried the drinks into the living area of her cozy apartment.

She sat on the sofa, relaxing, while Colin bent over the hearth to lit a fire in the fireplace. Memories of the two of them in college rushed back at her. The muscles in his back arched and strained against his shirt as he arranged the logs. She remembered how he smelled after working out at the college gym. The way he would chase her around his small apartment when his roommate was out and how they had made love all night long after attending that frat party.

Her heart fluttered as he rose and stepped away from the fireplace. God, the memories overwhelmed her and that small flame she had tried to ignore suddenly burst into an inferno.

How long had it been since she'd had sex? How long had it been since she'd even felt the stirrings of desire that now vibrated along her inner thighs?

But her daughter slept just down the hall.

She drank her glass of wine in one giant gulp. She still had feelings for this man, and she wasn't ready to face them. The thought of the two of them together again was intoxicating.

Her memories of their one night together left her body sizzling. Years had passed since she'd felt such a surge of desire.

Brooke stood and walked into the kitchen where she poured herself another glass of wine, needing the encouragement the alcohol instilled.

She returned to the couch and sank onto the cushions. Colin came over and sat beside her. They sat in silence, watching the flames. She placed her glass on the table and turned to him, pushing all thoughts from her mind, focused on the one thing she wanted. Him.

He looked at her, a quizzical expression on his face as

she reached for him.

She put her lips on his. His hands came up and wrapped around her face, holding her to him as his lips plundered hers.

The familiar magic smacked her in the middle, and she knew she'd come home. What was it about this man that made her body tingle in all the right places? Why had she not felt this familiar magic with anyone else?

Her arms wound around his neck, and she all but crawled on his lap, needing to be closer. She wanted this. She wanted to experience Colin again and see if the memories of them together in the past were as potent as she remembered.

Dizzy from the alcohol, her skin tingled as Colin's hand slid down her neck, her chest while his lips plundered hers.

A moan escaped her as heat radiated through her. Her body burned from the inside out, and her head began to spin. She pushed away from Colin and opened her eyes.

Her head lolled back on the couch. All the wine she'd consumed held her in its grip, leaving the room spinning wildly.

Colin watched her, breathing heavily. "You know the last time we were together, someone had spiked the punch, and we were both drunk. That night we created Olivia. And as much as I want you, and oh God, I want you so bad, you have no idea, the next time we have sex, I want us both sober."

Brooke shook her head, disappointment surging through her. "I'm sorry. I don't drink much. I was nervous tonight."

"Are you okay?"

"No. The room is spinning like crazy."

"Come on. Let me get you to bed."

"Alone?"

"Alone."

Colin stood and held out his hand. Brooke took his

hand and the room tilted. "Oh dear."

He held onto her, and together they walked to her bedroom.

"Where are your night clothes?"

Not certain what he intended, she glanced at him before she answered. "On the back of the bathroom door."

He led her to her bathroom door. "Is your robe in there?"

"Yes," she said, still uncertain.

"You get dressed for bed, and I'll wait to tuck you in. I want to make certain you're okay," he reassured her.

"I'm fine. I can take it from here," she said and pulled away from him. The room spun, and she almost lost her balance.

"Yeah, you're fine all right. I can wait out here until you're ready or I can help you get dressed for bed. Which do you prefer?"

"Alright, I'll get ready," she answered.

Brooke went into the bathroom and firmly closed the door behind her. It felt awkward as she washed her face, brushed her teeth, and put her nightgown on. Once her robe was firmly tied around her waist, she opened the door. "See? I'm all right."

"Yeah, well wait until you get those bed spins."

The thought nauseated her.

"I'm okay. I should walk you to the door."

"No, you should get in bed. I'll show myself to the door. After you crawl in bed."

She felt uneasy with him standing in her bedroom fully clothed. Yet this was the man whose bones she'd wanted to jump ten minutes ago. The room tilted, and she hurried to the bed. She never wanted to drink another glass of wine. And never more than one ever again.

He turned his back as she dropped her robe to the floor and then scurried beneath the covers.

"All set?" he asked.
"I think so."
"Do I need to put a trash can close to your side?"
"No."
"Are you going to be okay?"
"Yes, you can leave now."
"Goodnight, Brooke."
"Goodnight, Colin. Thanks."
"No problem."

Colin walked out of her bedroom and into the living area. The fire glowed in the hearth, and he frowned. How could he leave Brooke and Olivia sleeping in the apartment with the fireplace blazing?

Too many unattended flames became house fires. He glanced at Brooke's couch and grabbed a few pillows. At least he'd be close by if either one of them needed him. Though he was certain Brooke would not be too happy to learn he'd slept on her couch.

Chapter Eleven

Devon stood in Brooke's apartment, staring at Colin asleep on her couch. The man's spunk seemed to have drained from his body with the knowledge he had a daughter. Since he'd learned of Olivia, the competitive edge that Colin lived and worked by needed sharpening.

Colin needed to drop this good-guy act that had him sleeping on couches and taking care of drunken women and injured children. Devon had to give Colin a jolt to remind him why money and winning this competition were important.

A sparkling essence announced Gabriella's arrival. Just what he didn't need.

"Hey Devon, what's up?"

She came into full view, her angel attire a white nun's habit. She gazed at Colin. "Isn't that the sweetest picture? He stayed to take care of both of them."

She turned and smiled at Devon.

"That outfit is a little tame for you. Did you escape the convent?" he asked.

"No, I'm on my way to an exorcism and wanted to blend in with the others," she said. The smile on her angelic face almost blinded him with its radiance.

Devon shrugged. "Tell the demon I said hello."

"No way. I'm there for moral support for the priest. Nothing more."

She watched Colin sleeping peacefully. "I'm so pleased he's getting to know his daughter."

"They don't have much time left together," Devon threatened.

"Leave them alone, Devon. They're finding themselves again. He still has time to change."

Devon quietly contemplated how he could rock Colin's world again. "He's forgotten about work. He's forgotten about the million-dollar salary waiting for him in California. He's forgotten the very reason he hates Christmas."

"Great! We're making progress."

"I need him focused on work, not a five-year-old kid."

Gabriella rolled her eyes. "You insisted on him learning about his daughter. Now he's getting to know her. You're mad because this hasn't turned out like you planned."

"I don't care who she is. I should have killed her."

Gabriella gasped. "Oh, Devon, why do you need to hurt children?" Gabriella asked. "They're innocent. Leave them alone."

"They're tools in the game of life. But don't worry, I've already played the Olivia card." He shrugged. "There are other ways to affect Colin McDermott," he said, wondering what he could do grab Colin's attention.

Gabriella reached out and blew a palmful of dust in Colin's direction.

"What the hell did you just do?" Devon said, staring at Gabriella with his mouth wide in astonishment. "You can't do that. It's against the rules."

Her wings fluttered, and she smiled. "Oh yes, I can. I protected the three of them for the next twenty-four hours. I have to be at the exorcism, so until I return, they're safe."

"Damn you, Gabriella." He threw a blast of fire at Colin and an invisible shield protected the man. The flame extinguished on contact.

"Oh, stop your whining. Your nastiness can wait another day. Now I must be going...ta ta, Devon. See you soon."

The sparkling essence disappeared, leaving Devon to glare at Colin. "Life's a bitch, pal, and she can only protect you for so long."

~

Brooke woke with a pounding headache, a dry mouth and a burgeoning sense of shame. Why in the hell had she drunk so much? Spending the day buying presents for Olivia had seemed unreal. The two of them shopping for their daughter made it seem too much like they were a family. And it scared the hell out of her.

All the dreams she'd kept at bay were there in front of her with Colin by her side. She'd been unable to cope with the fact that she longed for her daughter to have what Brooke had experienced growing up—a mother and a father, a warm family environment.

After spending the day with Colin, she'd remembered how much fun they had together. How her body hummed with awareness at his touch. How she loved gazing into his deep, brown eyes to see them laughing with her. How his voice sent a shiver down her spine.

She'd hungered to experience Colin again. The touch of his hands on her, his mouth on her lips, and him deep inside her. God help her, but he was doing all the appropriate things to win her heart again, and yet his job could move him to California.

Sure, there were questions about his past that she'd never considered before. His reasons for not wanting children were still unclear. What had happened to his mother? Where was his father? Had he really been homeless?

Yet even with these questions, her heart tugged at her to forgive the past and move forward. To consider a possible future with Colin. And that thought frightened her.

Was she ready to share her daughter completely with him? Was she ready to give him a second chance?

She threw back the covers, needing to escape the musings of her mind and prepare for the day ahead. She needed to wake Olivia, feed her breakfast, dress her child and herself before they went shopping for a Christmas tree.

And with her pounding head, she needed aspirin and food. She tugged on her robe, made the bed and then opened the door to her bedroom. Funny, she didn't remember closing the door last night. She always left it open in case Olivia needed her.

Stepping into the hall that led to the living area of her apartment, she heard voices. Giggles. Her daughter was awake, but whom was she talking to?

Brooke came around the corner and saw Colin standing in her kitchen in the same clothes he'd worn the night before. His hair had a spike on top as if it hadn't been washed this morning. His face was unshaven. And then it slammed her. He'd never gone home.

"Good morning," he said.

"Good morning," she responded, not certain how to handle this situation in front of her daughter. She should be angry with him for sleeping over without her permission. She glanced into the living room and saw he'd found a blanket. He'd obviously slept on her couch.

"I decided to stay last night in case you or Olivia woke up and needed me."

She didn't respond.

"Mommy, Colin is fixing us breakfast."

"I see that."

"Do you like pancakes and eggs?" he asked.

"Yes," she said tentatively, still not certain of her response to Colin.

He stepped closer to her so that only she heard his voice. "I was afraid you wouldn't hear Olivia if she woke in the middle of the night or that you might need me."

"If *someone* had left my door open, I would have heard her just fine," she said.

"I didn't shut the door until she woke me this morning. We were letting you sleep a little longer," he said quietly.

"And how did you explain to my daughter why you

slept on the couch?" she asked, unable to stop staring at him despite her headache.

"I told her the truth. That last night you weren't feeling well, and I stayed to make certain the two of you were okay."

"Oh."

"Mom, are you okay?" Olivia asked.

"I'm fine, sweetie. How about you?"

"I'm hungry. We have to eat and get ready. We're going to the Christmas Tree Farm today."

Brooke stared at Colin, unsure, yet part of her was melting at the way he looked all tousled in the morning. God, what was she doing? This man had broken her heart in the past, and yet here he was early in the morning, standing in her kitchen and looking more delicious than a person had a right to.

He'd spent the night to take care of her and Olivia. He was definitely trying to earn that Boy Scout badge for good behavior.

Olivia hopped down from her chair and padded over to stand next to them. She looked up at each of the adults as if she could sense the tension in the air. "Let's cook breakfast guys. I'm hungry. We are going to the tree farm today, aren't we?"

Brooke felt lost seeing the warmth reflected from Colin's warm brown eyes. Olivia tugged on her robe to get her attention. "Mommy, we're still going, right?"

"Yes, Olivia, if Colin still wants to, we're going."

Colin smiled at Brooke. "Then we'd better finish our pancakes so we can get ready."

"Yeah," Olivia said, running around the kitchen. "Yeah."

"Not too much sugar," Brooke said softly to Colin. "She's already excited this morning."

He smiled. "God, you are so beautiful in the morning."

Brooke felt her cheeks flame, a warm flush filling her body. "You're not too bad looking yourself."

"Come on, let's eat," Olivia said.

"Fire up the stove. I think we'd better start cooking," Brooke said, her body so in tune with his she could hardly stand it.

"I'm already hot," Colin replied with a naughty smile.

~

Colin watched his daughter run from tree to tree, ooh-ing and ah-ing at each one. He tried not to care. He didn't want to care, but somehow she was working her way into his heart. A man wasn't supposed to know fear, yet he took one look at Olivia and was consumed with the emotion. What if there was an accident and something happened to him and Brooke?

What if…he couldn't let anything bad befall them. He just couldn't. No child should ever experience what he'd gone through with his mother only to be left behind at his grandmother's.

He pushed the sadness away, refusing to think of those memories here at the tree farm, where kids were having fun. Harried parents tried to find the perfect tree, for the perfect Christmas, to go with the perfect gifts for their perfect families.

Not the gift of a mother leaving her child. He hated Christmas. He hated Santa, lights, and decorated trees. Yet here he stood, a smile on his face, while Brooke and Olivia picked out a tree. And surprisingly, it wasn't as bad as he'd expected.

Brooke tried to convince Olivia to make a decision, but the little girl hurried to pine after another, not convinced she'd found the right one.

Last night he'd turned down sex with Brooke. Turned her down and gone to sleep on her couch instead of wrapped around her in her bed. What was wrong with him? How many men said no to sex, even with an inebriated woman?

Why was it crucial they both be sober the next time they had sex? Because she was the mother of his child? God that made him sound like such a dope. So what? Who cared? He didn't want forever with Brooke. It was just sex.

Wasn't it?

But Brooke got to him. Something about her made him yearn to throw her down in the snow and slowly remove their clothes to see if they were as good together as he remembered.

What about this woman tied him up in knots? Even in college he'd known she was special. Someone who understood him. Who just being with made him happy. Like today. Buying a Christmas tree would have been torture before, but somehow being with Brooke made it easier.

While she and Olivia were way ahead of him searching for the perfect tree, every few minutes Brooke glanced back and searched him out. When she did, their gazes would affix.

That connection, whatever it was, tied them together in ways that nothing with anyone else ever had. He felt linked to her in ways that social media could never achieve.

So, what now? How did they go from here? And when would Brooke let him tell Olivia he was her father? Time was running out. He longed to know his daughter better before he left town. He demanded that she realize her father had never abandoned or not wanted her. He'd just never known of her.

"Colin, Colin, come quick," Olivia cried. "We found it."

He hurried and caught up with her and Brooke. "Wow, that's a beauty. It's not too tall, is it?"

Brooke smiled. "I told her the same thing. But I think once they cut off the trunk, it'll be fine."

"Will it fit in the car?" Olivia asked her eyes wide with wonder.

"We'll tie it on top," Colin remarked, looking the tree over.

"But won't it get broken?"

"No, they'll tie netting around it."

"Oh," she said staring at the tree. "It's really pretty."

She started to jump up and down with excitement. "We'll take it home and decorate it, and then we can put presents under it, and then Santa will come with my new puppy."

Colin and Brooke exchanged a glance. Colin shook his head at Brooke. He hadn't encouraged her, but Olivia was determined that Santa was bringing her a puppy.

"Let me find a salesman, and we'll buy us a tree."

"Yeah."

"Colin, I'll buy it," Brooke said.

He shook his head. "Nope. I'm getting the tree. You're supplying the decorations."

After loading the tree on the top of the car, they began the hour drive from the farm to the city. In a matter of minutes, Olivia fell fast asleep in the back seat.

Colin glanced at her in the rearview mirror. Her head was laid over in her booster chair, her purse clutched tightly in her hand. Olivia was all girl. She could play rough, but she was going to be a girly girl.

He glanced at her mother. If she grew up to look like Brooke, boys could be a problem. And where would Colin be during that time of her life? Would Brooke eventually marry someone who would take his place in Olivia's life? That thought galvanized him.

"When can I tell her I'm her father?"

"When I think she's ready. Look at her, she's still

recovering from that awful wreck."

"Yes, but I'm leaving soon," Colin said, trying to quell the frustration edging into his voice.

"And that concerns me. You want to tell her you're her father and then disappear? That's not really fair to her," Brooke responded, her mouth tense, her eyes wide with fright.

"I can't help it. My goal is to win this promotion," he told her. "I've worked all year toward being named western sales director."

Brooke raised her brows at him. "Then don't let us stop you. Win the promotion and move to California, but I'm not going to upset my daughter by letting you hurt her."

"She's our daughter."

"For now, she's my daughter."

Colin gripped the steering wheel more tightly, frustration surging through him. The wreck had happened barely a week ago, and they all needed time to adjust. But how long before Brooke gave him permission to tell Olivia the truth?

Brooke stared out the window, biting her lip, deep in thought. Finally she turned back to him.

"About last night…" she said.

Colin peeked at her. "What about it?"

Her cheeks were rosy. "I should never have come on to you. It's been so long…"

Colin tried to keep his eyes on the road. The woman was exasperating at times. "Just because I turned you down last night doesn't mean I don't want to sleep with you. Last night was incredibly hard for me," he said with a sigh. "But the next time we're together, I want both of us sober and unable to keep our hands off each other."

"You're not just here because of Olivia?" Brooke asked.

"Hell, no," he said too loudly. "I wanted you before I knew about Olivia."

Brooke's brows rose in surprise.

"Look, this thing between us may not last, and I'm here to get to know my daughter. But there was an *us* before Olivia, and I want to find out if this thing we have is real or fleeting."

Brooke smiled at him. "Thanks. I'm glad."

They drove through the countryside in silence as the trees whizzed by. Snow began to fall and a sense of peace enveloped the car. Colin enjoyed Brooke's company even with the dreaded Christmas music filling the car.

"You told me you haven't seen your mother, but how did that make you decide you never wanted children?" Brooke asked, breaking the quiet.

He took a deep breath. "My childhood was not the greatest."

"A lot of people have bad childhoods, but that doesn't stop them from having kids."

"No, you're right."

Colin drove on, not saying anything, trying to think of some way to tell her without evoking her pity. He didn't need her pity.

"Things happen in this life that adults have no control over, but children are at the mercy of their parents. I never wanted to risk putting a child in that situation."

"So you were put in a bad situation?"

"Not after I went to live with my grandmother. No child of mine will do without food and shelter."

"Olivia never has, and as long as there is breath in my body, she never will," Brooke assured him.

He turned and smiled at her, hoping he could lead the conversation in a direction other than his past. "I know that now. But I didn't then. You're a great mother to her. I see how much you love her."

Brooke smiled. "Thanks. I was afraid at first that you would try to take her from me."

Colin shook his head. "Never, unless you didn't take good care of her."

"So what are we going to do? How do we handle this situation without hurting her?" Brooke asked.

"I'm not worried so much about her getting hurt as I am about one of us being hurt," Colin said.

Brooke gazed at him, her expression quizzical. "What do you mean?"

"I'm afraid that if I go to California, you'll find some man to take my place. I'll come home to find you happily married and Olivia with a replacement father."

Brooke laughed. "You're concerned about me finding a replacement father?"

"Yes," he said, strangely hurt. This wasn't particularly funny.

"I haven't married, dated, or hardly even flirted for the last five years, and now you're concerned about a replacement father. I'm sorry, but that's funny. My father was even harassing me the other day because I don't date. I bet the same can't be said for you. How many women have you dated in the last five years?"

"A few, but mainly I work. I work almost seven days a week."

"You haven't these last few days," Brooke said.

"I know, and tomorrow that has to end. I have to refocus on the next sale. I've sold one hospital, but I have two hospitals I'm waiting to hear from and one appointment scheduled for next week. I should have at least three appointments lined up. I haven't been as focused."

Brooke stared at him, her brow a worried frown. "I'm sorry, but yet I'm glad you've been here. It's meant a lot to me."

Colin smiled as warmth spread through him. "Thanks. Me too."

"Are we nearly there yet?" came a sleepy voice from

the back.

"I'm taking the exit to your house. You better wake up and get ready to decorate the tree," Colin said.

He glanced at Brooke, noticing the way her sweater fit snugly over her breasts. "We're telling her soon," he said quietly.

Chapter Twelve

Brooke sat at her desk, gazing at a painting of the Colorado Rockies on her office wall. All morning she'd tried to focus, but images of Olivia and Colin decorating the tree, laughing together while they tossed foil icicles on each other, had intruded.

What was she doing? Her daughter adored Colin. How would she react to the news that Colin was her father? And how would Olivia handle him moving to California and disappearing from their lives once again?

The thoughts churned inside her, and underneath it all she wondered what her life would be like if she'd told Colin she was pregnant. Would they have gotten married? Would he have wanted the baby?

The questions were endless, and somehow she didn't know the answers to anything right now. No matter how hard she tried, she couldn't concentrate on the year-end balance sheets.

All she could think about was Colin. The way he made her laugh. The way his kisses made her body tingle in forgotten places. The way he made her heart do a little shimmy at the sight of him.

Part of her wanted him, and part of her wanted to grab Olivia by the hand and run.

A knock at her door returned her focus. "Come in," she called, trying to appear busy.

"Hey you," Amelia said, opening the door. "How was your weekend?"

She nodded. "It was okay."

Amelia's eyes widened. "Just okay? You were going shopping with our very hot Santa."

"Yes, we did some shopping."

"And?" she asked. "Details. I need details. Since I have

no man in my life, I'm living vicariously through you."

"Ha! You're not getting much action then, are you?"

"None, to be exact."

"Don't look to me," Brooke said, shrugging her shoulders. "I didn't see any either."

"Oh, come on. No spit swapping, nothing?"

"I have a five-year-old."

"Even five-year-olds have to sleep sometime." She paused for a moment. "So you went shopping and then he left?"

Brooke shook her head. "No. We went shopping, and then we went to dinner."

"So how was that?"

Brooke smiled at the memory of the two of them talking and laughing over dinner. It'd been fun. "He's different than he was when we were in college. He's deeper. There's more substance to him than just a kid who wanted to graduate."

Amelia's brows rose. "Well, thank God for that. Are you the same person you were in college?"

"No. But he's working toward a promotion. A promotion that will take him to California, away from me and Olivia," Brooke said, realizing she didn't want him to leave. She wanted him to stay.

"Palm trees, warm weather…sounds dreadful." Amelia said. "What's really bothering you about Colin?"

Brooke tensed. "He turned down sex with me."

"What?"

A laugh escaped from Brooke. "That would never have happened in college. I'd had a little too much wine Saturday night. The excuse he gave was he wanted us to both be sober the next time we had sex."

"Oh my God. How many men turn down sex with a woman? Especially a drunk one," Amelia said, her blue eyes wide with surprise.

"Not many," Brooke said. She should be glad he'd turned her down, but disappointment made her shoulders slump.

"The man must be a saint."

"Hardly. But he's different. He's not the same man I knew in college. I like him so much better, but I'm scared of him. Olivia is *my* daughter, and suddenly he's in her life, and he wants to be involved. He wants to buy her Christmas presents, start a college fund, and make certain she's taken care of."

Amelia stared at her as if she'd lost her mind.

"And this bothers you why? He's certainly no deadbeat father. I may give him volunteer of the year just because he's awoken the woman in you."

Brooke laughed. "That frightens me most of all. I don't want to care about him and then have him get on a plane and fly away."

"Have you ever considered you could go with him?" Amelia asked.

"That seems like such an impossibility. Leaving here and uprooting Olivia. Leaving behind my dad and my job for a man I'm still unsure of. No, that's not going to happen."

They sat for a long moment of silence. Finally Amelia said, "Let's think about this from his perspective. He suddenly has a daughter he never knew of. The woman he cared for in college is back in his life, and he's trying to win a big promotion. The man must be under a tremendous amount of stress, yet he's made time for you and Olivia."

"He didn't have to."

"No, but he has."

Brooke shook her head. "Did I tell you he looked for me after I left college? He tried to find me."

Amelia raised her brows and shook her head. "You two are really pissing me off. You both need to wake up and drink the coffee. If you'd both quit being so afraid, maybe you'd realize you're still attracted and just let nature take its course. If you let this man walk out of your life without taking a chance, you're going to regret missing this opportunity. I'm not saying start picking out a china pattern, but girl, if you like him, then give him a chance."

"I wanted to have sex with him."

"Give up the alcohol," Amelia said.

"Done."

"Relax, what's the worst that could happen?"

"I could harm my kid by letting her get to know her father and then him disappearing from our life," Brooke said, feeling a little indignant.

Amelia's brows drew together in a frown. "Are you worried about Olivia or yourself?"

The truth slapped her in the face. Oh my God. "Both, but mainly me."

~

Colin had driven into Denver. He walked into the office and checked in for the first time since last Friday, when he'd picked up the new client in Greenwood.

He checked the sales board where they posted their numbers. He had one sale and Logan had…shit! The man had two sales.

The door opened, and his nemesis strolled in, grinning like the Publishers Clearing House had delivered a hefty check. "Hey, Colin, how's it going?"

"Great!" he lied. "I'm just about to leave for a sales call."

"Oh yeah, who are you bagging this time?"

"I'd rather not say just yet."

Logan grinned. "I see you made a sale on Friday. Congratulations."

"Thanks."

"Of course you're still down by one, and I'm on my way with contracts and to pick up a check myself."

"You sold another one?" Colin asked in disbelief.

"Wrapping her up today," he said, smiling. "Hey, how's that Santa gig going for you? Has the big man gotten the contract on that account yet?" Logan said with a laugh.

"I'm still working on it."

Logan slapped him on the back. "I thought about trying out that Santa angle at Mother Francis Hospital, but the nuns frowned when I mentioned it."

"I didn't offer to be Santa. I was coerced into playing the part. And if it gets me that sale, it will be one of the largest accounts in this area. One you'll have a hard time overcoming," Colin said with pretend confidence.

Logan shrugged. "Yeah, well, I don't see that number up on the sales board yet."

"Their board meets this week. Until then, there are other fish in the sea," he said with a smile.

"Yeah, I know. But I wouldn't go any further north in Colorado. I've hit every hospital in the northern part of the state. That's why you didn't see me last week. So where have you been prospecting?" he asked.

A surge of disappointment flowed through Colin. He'd planned on heading up north last week. But last week, his life had been torn asunder, and he'd spent most of his time with Brooke and Olivia. Not out cold-calling.

"Thanks, I wasn't going that direction anyway," he lied.

"The big announcement is less than two weeks away. After today, I'll be two sales up on you. Warm, sunny California is only days away," he said, a smirk on his face.

"Don't pack your bags yet. I don't hear the fat lady singing," Colin warned.

Logan laughed. "Gotta run, Colin. Who's eating dust now?"

He walked out of the room, and Colin stood there,

stunned. He'd let his personal life get in the way of his job, and now everything he'd dreamed of was in jeopardy of slipping away.

Colin had to get back on the road today. Right now. He had to call on every account in his backlog files of anyone who might reconsider. He had his work cut out for him if he still wanted this promotion.

The image of Brooke danced in his mind. He had to concentrate on work or risk losing the advancement.

And then he remembered he'd agreed to go to Olivia's doctor's exam tomorrow.

~

Colin was late. He'd spent the morning contacting clients he'd presented to in the past, and the phone calls resulted in two appointments. Maybe this time he could convince them their hospital needed his product.

Right now he was rushing to meet Brooke at Olivia's pediatrician.

The doors to the office complex swished open as he ran inside. He saw Olivia and Brooke sitting, reading a book. He hurried over to them.

"Hi," he said.

Brooke glanced up at him, her reception cool. "Hi."

"You're late, Colin," Olivia said, swinging her legs over the edge of the chair.

"I'm sorry, Olivia. Work got in the way."

"Your work gets you in trouble."

Colin couldn't help but grin at the kid. "Yes, Olivia, it does."

"Why don't you quit?"

"Because I like my job," he said, and he did. He loved the challenge of making quota, finding new clients, and convincing them to buy his product.

"Olivia Warren," a nurse called.

"Come on," Brooke said, standing and taking Olivia by the hand.

"We've got to do something about that name," Colin said under his breath.

Brooke turned and glared at him. He mouthed silently to her, "She's my daughter."

Colin followed behind them. First they stopped at a scale, where Olivia was weighed, and then they checked her temperature.

Soon they were sitting inside an examination room, waiting for the doctor. Colin sat in a chair out of the way while Brooke helped Olivia into a gown. Colin turned his head. She was his daughter, but until Olivia knew, he didn't want her to feel uncomfortable. Hell, he felt awkward. This was a whole new experience for him, having a daughter.

He glanced around the typical examination room with the cabinets and plastic boxes on the wall. Pamphlets on the flu, diabetes, and measles filled plastic bins.

He glanced at his watch. His next appointment was in ninety minutes. This couldn't take long.

"Do you need to be somewhere," Brooke asked. "You know you didn't have to come today."

"I have awhile before my next appointment. And I wanted to be here to make certain she's okay," he said, wishing he hadn't agreed to come but not wanting Brooke to know.

"I could have told you."

"I know, but I wanted to hear what the doctor said."

Brooke gave him a glance that insinuated he was a liar, but he ignored her.

"How's that Christmas tree looking, Olivia?"

"Oh, it's so pretty. Now I can't wait to get my puppy."

Brooke frowned at her daughter. "Santa is not bringing you a dog."

Olivia shrugged. "You say that, but I'm still talking to

Santa."

Brooke shook her head. They sat in the exam room for ten minutes. Colin glanced at his watch again.

Where the hell was that doctor? Why couldn't they be on time?

"If you need to go, it's okay," Brooke said."

"No, I'm staying," Colin replied. "Have you heard back from the members of the board yet?"

"What?" Brooke asked, confusion spreading across her face.

"You know, on the software that I sell. I really need that sale."

"No one has said anything. We have a meeting scheduled for next week. It will be discussed and a decision made then," she said, looking perplexed.

"Oh, I thought it was this week," Colin said, wishing it were a week earlier. He needed that sale.

"It was delayed until right before the holidays."

Colin glanced at his watch again. He needed to be on the road and working this afternoon. Where was the doctor?

He stood and started to pace in the small room. Brooke watched him, her brows drawn together in a frown. "Why are you so edgy today?"

He ran his hand through his hair. "Logan is two sales ahead of me. I've got to focus on making more sales."

"Instead of being with us," Brooke said.

Colin glanced at her. "No, that's not what I meant. If I intend to win this promotion, I should see as many clients a day as possible."

"Instead of being with us." She said it again.

"I'm trying to do both. I'm here, aren't I?" he said trying to keep the exasperation from his voice.

Brooke frowned at him. "Yes, but you're driving me crazy. Your pacing is wearing out the floor. It's obvious you want to be somewhere else. You can leave."

"It's just that I have an appointment in sixty minutes, and we're sitting here waiting for the doctor."

"Then go. If you need to leave, it's okay. I've handled her being sick all of her life."

"That's not my fault," Colin responded, his voice rising.

Brooke's brows rose, and she glanced over at Olivia before her gaze returned to Colin's.

Olivia watched them. "Are you two fighting?"

Colin took a deep breath. "No, Olivia. I'm anxious today. It's not your Mom's fault, it's mine."

"What's anxious?" she asked, struggling with the word.

Brooke shook her head and rolled her eyes just as the doctor walked through the door.

"Hi, there. Sorry, I'm late," he said, smiling at them. "Miss Olivia, let's see how those stitches look."

Colin sat down in the chair and watched as the doctor examined her abdomen. The incision was longer than he'd imagined, and the stitches were a painful reminder of how close she'd come to dying before he ever knew her. He felt his blood pressure climb at the thought of never knowing Olivia.

He didn't care what Brooke thought. He was going to tell Olivia he was her father just as soon as they were together alone.

"I'm going to remove the stitches. It shouldn't hurt. You let me know if you feel any pain," the doctor said, smiling at Olivia.

In less than five minutes, the stitches were all out.

"She's doing great. I'd like to see her once more in about two weeks, but if she continues to do well, I'll release her."

Brooke sighed. "Thank you."

"Miss Olivia, I'd still like you to avoid any jungle gyms. Let's get over this before you start swinging like a monkey."

"If I get a puppy, I can play with him, right?"

The doctor smiled. "Just don't let his claws scratch your side."

"It's not a problem. She doesn't have a dog."

"Doctor, do you have a dog?" Olivia asked.

He smiled. "I have two dachshunds."

"Santa's bringing me a puppy."

Brooke shook her head at Olivia, but she didn't say anything.

"You all have a Merry Christmas," the doctor said as he went out the door.

Colin glanced at his watch, his frustration at an all-time high. This was the first time he'd seen Olivia's stitches, and it scared the hell out of him. He'd almost never gotten to meet his daughter.

He glared at Brooke. She was dressing Olivia. "What?"

"I didn't know the surgical scar was so deep."

Brooke nodded. "Thank God you were there that day."

Her words made his blood pressure climb even higher, and he resisted the urge to create a scene in front of Olivia.

"I should have known about her before that day."

"Can we please talk about this later," Brooke said, her gaze pointing towards Olivia.

"Time is running out," Colin said and walked out the door.

~

Brooke drove to her father's home, trying to keep her emotions together, realizing how angry she felt toward Colin and even Olivia. She refused to give up on this idea of a dog. And she was not getting a puppy for Christmas no matter what. No dog.

Olivia sensed her mood and sat in her chair in the back of the car, silent for most of the trip.

"Mommy, why can't I go back to school today?"

"Because I want you to rest. The doctor took out your stitches, and you don't need to be roughhousing with the other kids. Besides, you enjoy spending time with Grandpa."

"Yeah, but I wanted to see if Santa was there today."

"Why?" Brooke asked, suddenly suspicious.

"I need to talk to him."

"Olivia, you're not getting a dog for Christmas."

"But I want a puppy."

"You're five. You're not getting a dog."

"Santa's going to bring me one."

"Santa brings what I tell him to bring, and he's not bringing you a dog," Brooke said, frustration overwhelming her.

For a moment Olivia didn't respond, and Brooke thought the tantrum was over.

"Colin will bring me a dog," Olivia said defiantly.

Brooke pulled into her father's driveway and didn't say a word. She parked the car, got out, and removed Olivia from her car seat.

"Are you mad, Mommy?"

"No," Brooke said. "But, I'm no longer discussing the dog with you. You're not getting one. We're done."

Olivia started to cry. Brooke took her by the hand and led her up the steps to her father's house.

She rang the bell. When he opened the front door, Brooke felt like crying too but knew that would alarm him.

"Hey, what's wrong?" he asked as he bent down to Olivia's level.

"I want a dog," Olivia cried.

Her father glanced at her, and Brooke shook her head. "Don't say anything."

"How about I put in a movie about dogs and you can watch that?" he said as he stood.

"Okay," Olivia said, walking into the house.

He followed her into the living room, where he started the movie. Soon, Olivia was lying on the floor watching television.

Brooke walked into the yellow kitchen with red accents. She sank down at the table and her father joined her.

"Tough day?" he asked.

Tears pricked her eyes. "You can say that."

"What brought on the tears about the dog?"

Brooke explained to him how Olivia would not give up on the idea of getting a dog.

"It's the first of many battles with her, honey," her father said. "Remember how you wanted a kitten?"

The memory of crying and begging for a kitten came back to her. "Oh yeah, I'd forgotten."

She sighed. "Even Colin is angry with me today. When we went to the doctor he saw how badly she was hurt, he got angry. Colin said he should have known about her before that day."

Her dad hugged her. "Honey, think if you were in his shoes. How would you have felt, not knowing about Olivia?"

"I did what I thought was best."

"I know, but you're going to have to give him some time. He's angry. I can't imagine not being with you the first five years of your life. I can't imagine not seeing your first step or your first tooth. Hearing you say 'daddy'. I wish things were different, but I wouldn't think much of him as a man if he weren't a little put out with you."

"Oh, Dad," she said. "You're not making me feel any better. In fact, you're making me feel like crap."

"I'm sorry."

"He's pressuring me, Dad. He wants to tell Olivia he's her father. He wants to spend time with her. He's set up a college fund, and he's paying child support. Crap, he's doing all the right things, and me—I—don't know if I want to share my daughter with him."

Her father reached out and squeezed her hand. "You've had her all to yourself for all these years."

"I know."

"He's missed out on so much," her father said.

"I know that, too. I never thought I'd feel guilty, but I do. I keep wondering if we'll somehow damage Olivia when we tell her he's her father."

"That's nonsense. She's a resilient kid."

"What should I do, Dad? What do I do?"

"You give Colin some time. When you feel ready, you tell Olivia he's her father."

"I'm not ready for her to know."

"Colin has the right to get to know his daughter. He's already missed out on years with her, so you need to prepare yourself, because soon, she's going to know."

"But what about me? What about the fact that I'm scared of trusting him again with not only my heart, but Olivia's? What if this time he hurts both of us?"

Chapter Thirteen

Colin walked out of the doctor's office, furious. This cat-and-mouse game with Brooke had to stop. The next time they were together, they were telling Olivia. He didn't care what Brooke thought. Olivia was his daughter, too. Committed to Olivia, he wanted her to know he was her father.

Yet, he'd never had a father figure in his life. And memories of his early childhood were not the best. But Olivia wasn't going to have to live without her father. Could he be a decent father? Could he give Olivia the love and attention that his own parents had been unable to give him? Why had his mother never returned? For many years he'd wondered, but never pursued the answer, afraid of what he'd learn.

Where had his father been? He needed answers.

After his appointment he drove like a mad man, doing twenty miles over the speed limit, eager to learn the truth. He'd been a coward for so many years, afraid of what he'd learn about his mother and why his father had left him. Around the age of seven, he'd realized his mother would never return, and he'd stopped asking questions.

So why had his mother left, and who was his father?

It took him over an hour to reach the nursing home where his grandmother lived. The automatic doors swished open as he walked through them. The smell of sick, elderly people assaulted his nose, making him uncomfortable.

When he walked into her room, she sat in her wheelchair, reading a book. She glanced up when he walked in.

"Colin, what are you doing here? Are you all right?"

He leaned down and kissed her on the cheek. "Yes and no," he said, rising and staring at her. "I need some answers."

"What?" she said, her eyes wide with wonder.

"What happened to my mother?"

His grandmother laid down her book, reached out, and took his hand. "I don't know."

"I need to know, Grandma. I need to know if I'm going to do the same thing to my kid."

"Your girlfriend is pregnant?"

He shook his head. "No, I recently learned I have a five-year-old daughter."

Colin quickly explained about Brooke and Olivia.

His grandmother's eyes teared. "A great-granddaughter. Colin, please bring her to see me. I'd love to meet her and Brooke."

"I will, Grandma, but first you have to tell me what happened. I don't want to make the same mistakes as my mother. I don't want my child to not know her parents," he said, prepared to hear the sordid details of his past.

"Oh, Colin," his grandmother replied, sniffling and shaking her head.

She reached behind her into a cabinet and pulled out an old picture album. She opened it to a picture of his mother as a baby.

"I can hardly stand to look at these pictures, yet I keep them close. Your mother was beautiful. In high school she was a member of the drill team and very popular."

She slowly turned the pages of the photo album, and he watched his mother change from a baby to a young girl in high school. He'd seen pictures of her, but he'd never seen this particular photo album.

"During her senior year, she met your father, Colin Ryan. He was a wild child. Drove a fast car, liked to drink, and ran with a troubled crowd. He pursued your mother and—against my better judgment—they began to date. She'd always been a good girl, never getting into trouble, so I tried not to worry. I thought he was a phase she'd outgrow."

Her hand stopped on a page, her fingers caressing the photo. His mother wore a formal dress with a corsage pinned to the satin, a smile on her beautiful face. A man stood beside her in a tux.

She stared at the photo. "This picture is the last photo of the two of them together, attending the homecoming dance."

A tear trickled down her cheek, and she wiped it away.

Colin wanted to grab the album and see his father, but waited.

"That night, Colin brought her home past her curfew. I was furious. I'd been waiting up for her return. We had an argument about them coming in late. I told him he could never see her again." She stopped and looked at the picture. Her voice lowered, "Afterwards he went to meet some of his friends. They were drinking. There was a drag car race on highway 49. He lost control and was killed instantly. Life was never the same for your mother."

"He never knew about me." Colin realized.

His grandmother shook her head. "No, six weeks later your mom realized she was pregnant. She was furious with me and blamed me for Colin's death. And believe me I've often wondered over the years if I ended his life by breaking them up."

"No, Grandma. He chose to race while he was drinking. That's not your fault."

"I know, but the events of that night sent your mother's life spinning out of control. If he hadn't gone in search of his friends, he would still be alive today," she said, her eyes distant and unfocused.

"You aren't responsible for the choice he made."

"Maybe not." But she didn't sound convinced.

"What did Mom do when she realized she was pregnant?"

"Against our better wishes, she quit school. When you were born, your grandfather and I offered to let her live at home and return to school. We would take care of you, and she could get her education. But she was angry. She thought the only man she would ever love had died because I said he couldn't see her anymore. So she moved out, taking you with her."

Colin shook his head, thinking of his mother, eighteen, with a baby, moving out of her parents' home.

"Where did she go? I mean, she had no money, no education, and a small baby."

"At first she moved in with some girlfriends. She would come to see us about every two-three months. We'd see how much you'd grown, and then she'd be gone. Sometimes she'd let me keep you while she hunted for a job. I know she was a waitress at a local diner for a while. Someone told me she had gotten involved with drugs, but I never knew that for certain."

"I don't remember drugs. I remember her working hard to make a living. She always had more than one job, yet I still went to bed at night hungry. We moved a lot. Several times we slept in homeless shelters. It's why I contribute my time to them even today."

His grandmother put her face in her hands. "I didn't know."

"So what happened that last time she brought me to your house? I know we've discussed this before, but I'm trying to understand. I need to know if we missed anything," he said, wanting to know what happened to his mother.

His grandmother stared at him in bewilderment. "We haven't spoken about this since you were a small boy. You refused to talk about her when she didn't return. You were angry. You didn't want to hear her name."

Colin paced the floor. "I hated her. She left me at your house on Christmas Eve and didn't come back."

"She loved you, Colin. Several times before, I'd tried to convince her to leave you with me while she got her life together, but she refused. She said you were her responsibility."

"Then where is she?" he asked his voice rising. "If she loved me, she would have come back."

"I don't know. I turned in a missing person's report, but they acted like she had just walked away. I searched for her. I even hired a private investigator. But no one could find her. The daughter I raised would never have gone off willingly and left you," his Grandmother said, her eyes filled with sadness.

"Do you think she was killed?"

"It's been over twenty years. There's no word of her. I think she's dead."

Colin sighed. Sadness welled up inside him. She was right. He had memories of his mother loving him. She would kiss him goodnight and say "it's just you and me, kid."

Something must have happened to her.

Life had dealt him the worst. A father who was killed the night he was conceived and a mother who had vanished.

Could he be a decent parent? He'd had no father, very few pleasant memories of his mother, and a grandmother who had done the best she could. His parenting examples were not great. Could he give Olivia the kind of love and care that a child needed?

"Most children think it's their fault when a parent leaves, which often is not true. Your father never knew about you, and your mother must be in heaven. You have a kind heart, a loving spirit, Colin, you'll make a great father," his grandmother said, staring into his eyes.

"But what if something happens to me?" he asked. The old anxiety returned now that he knew about his parents and how his life had been affected by unseen circumstances.

"Sometimes life is out of our control. You're a smart man. Do all that you can to shelter Olivia, but understand you can't stop every bad thing from happening to her. Your dad did not intend to die that night. He didn't know he had a child. And your Mom…I really think she planned on returning the night she left."

"But she brought all my clothes, all my belongings."

His grandmother sighed. "Yes, she did."

"Which makes me hate her all over again."

His grandmother reached out and grabbed his hand, squeezing it. "Don't hate her. It won't do any good."

"Then why did we come back to your house?

"It was the first Christmas after your grandfather had passed away. She planned to come home and spend the holidays with me. I thought she had finally forgiven me for your father's death, and I'd convince her to stay and get an education. I was filled with so much hope, and then she never returned. Do you remember the last thing she said to you?" she asked.

Colin had tried very hard to forget that night. He'd buried the pain of a small boy waiting for his mother's return deep in his psyche.

"Barely. I remember how she smelled. The sound of her voice and the way she would tuck me in at night."

His grandmother smiled. "She promised to return before Santa Claus came."

A painful wrench gripped his heart and now he understood even more why he hated Christmas. Why he hated Santa Claus. She'd broken her promise. But had it been intentional? He would probably never know.

Colin ran his hand through his hair. "Only she never came back."

"Do you understand why I think something happened to her?"

Unable to speak, he simply nodded. The woman he'd hated for so many years had probably died a gruesome death. And the father he'd wondered about had never known of him.

Colin's throat clogged with tears. "Can I see that picture of my father?"

His grandmother handed the photo to him. He stared into the eyes of a young man who smiled like he had the world in his hand. Dressed in a tux, with his arm around Colin's mother, the two appeared happy, not knowing their world would change forever that night.

He could see his features in his father's mouth and eyes. And when he looked at his mother's photo, he could see Olivia. "Olivia has mom's eyes and nose."

"Oh, Colin, please bring her to see me. I want to meet my great-granddaughter."

"I will, Grandma, just as soon as I tell her I'm her father. And believe me, she'll know very soon."

$\sim$

Colin had made up his mind. He was done. The time to tell Olivia was past due. Driving back toward Crystal Mountain, he pressed the number on his Bluetooth, and it rang Brooke's cell phone.

"Hi," she said.

"Hi," he responded.

"Are you still mad?"

He thought about it. No, he wasn't mad, but he wasn't going to let her put this off any longer. "No."

"Good. I'm sorry, Colin. We'll tell her soon."

"When is 'soon'?" he asked.

Brooke was silent for a moment. "Two weeks."

"No."

"What do you mean, 'no'? She's my daughter. I make all decisions regarding her welfare," Brooke said, the tension in her voice rising.

Colin took a deep breath. It would do no good to get angry. "She's *our* daughter. I want to tell her this weekend."

"That's too soon. She's already had so much drama in her life. I don't want her upset over this."

"Why are you stalling?" he asked, suddenly realizing this wasn't about Olivia.

"I just told you."

"You gave me a clinical response. I think she's a strong little girl. This isn't going to upset her."

"We're talking about a child. A child who hasn't had a father in her life for the first five years, who only recently has been asking about her father? Now suddenly you appear, and I'm supposed to let you tell her the truth? I don't think so. Not at first."

"So when?"

"Two weeks."

"I'm leaving in two weeks."

"We'll tell her right before you leave."

"Oh, that's going to make her feel better. Hi, I'm your dad, and now I'm leaving. See you in two months," he said, unable to keep the sarcasm out of his voice.

"I'm not ready to tell her."

"Aha, now the truth comes out. You're not ready to tell her the truth. You don't want to answer why I didn't know about her," Colin said, suddenly understanding Brooke's reluctance.

"That's not true."

"Sure it is. If it's not, tell me how you're going to explain why I never knew about her."

"I—crap, Colin. I don't know. I'm just not ready for her to learn about you."

"Okay," he relented. "But if we continue on, don't you think she's going to get suspicious?"

"Why would she?"

"Because she's a smart kid, and she's asking questions already. She's going to learn who I am before I leave," he said, unable to keep the defiant tone from his voice.

Chapter Fourteen

Friday night Brooke sat in the Italian restaurant with Colin and Olivia. Their heads bowed together as the two of them played some kind of game on his phone. Occasionally a giggle would erupt from Olivia, and Colin would smile.

Brooke was amazed at how patient Colin was with Olivia. He didn't let her get away with being mean, and he always managed to redirect her attention and somehow avoid the tantrum. He seemed to have a way with her daughter that she'd never expected. His parenting skills not only amazed her but frightened her.

How in the hell could he end up being the better parent when he hadn't wanted Olivia to begin with? It just didn't seem fair. Since the day Olivia was born, Brooke had worked with her, trying to give her advanced learning. Now Colin was the fun parent, playing games and entertaining her. Brooke tried to tell herself that when the newness wore off, Olivia would test him. Yet she couldn't help but feel a little jealous.

And that left her frustrated at herself. Why in the world should she be jealous of Colin? Olivia was *her* daughter.

When their pizza arrived at the table, Colin turned off the game. "Okay, Olivia, game time is over. We have to eat our food so we can go home and watch a Christmas movie."

Olivia frowned at him. "But I'm not hungry. I want to play the bird game."

"You need to eat your pizza. Even adults can't play games until they eat their dinner."

She picked up a piece of pizza and made a grimace. "I don't want it."

Colin picked up a piece and took a big bite into the gooey cheese. He chewed. "Mmmmm, my tummy really likes this pizza."

Brooke admired the way he handled an unusually tired and stubborn Olivia. Tonight she teetered on the edge of being a cranky little girl.

Olivia raised her brows at him, crossed her arms across her chest and said, "I bet my daddy wouldn't make me eat my pizza."

Brooke had to do everything she could not to choke on her food.

A scowl crossed Colin's face. He glanced at her, and she knew. The look he sent her told her without any words being said.

Oh no, he couldn't.

"No, Colin."

"It's time, Brooke. I'm done," he said.

Olivia glanced between the two of them, her little face wrinkled in confusion.

"No. I said no!" Brooke insisted, raising her voice, fear gripping her. She wanted to yank Olivia from the chair and run.

Colin turned from her, put his pizza back on his plate, and picked up Olivia's hand. "Olivia, I'm your father and I want you to eat your dinner. I didn't know you existed until your accident, or I would have been here watching you grow into a beautiful little girl."

Olivia glanced at her mother for confirmation and then back at Colin. Brooke gripped the table with both hands as anger surged through her. This was not the plan. They were supposed to wait until Brooke told Colin he could tell Olivia. Damn him!

Olivia giggled and held out her arms. Colin scooted closer to the table as she wrapped her arms around him and hugged him. "I'm glad. I just wish you would have found me sooner."

"Me too, baby. Me too," he said, his voice cracking as he looked up at the ceiling and blinked his eyes rapidly.

Brooke watched her daughter hug Colin and smile like it was just another day. Her anger dissipated. Her eyes filled with tears as she watched her daughter accept the news that Colin was her father. Her heart wrenched with guilt. She wanted to go back in time and hit the Redo button. She had screwed this up so badly.

"Will you live with us now?" Olivia asked.

Brooke wished the floor would open and help her disappear.

Colin smiled at her and glanced at Brooke.

Brooke jumped in. "We'll talk about that later."

"Will you come see me?" Olivia asked.

"As much as I can," he answered.

"Will you come to my school and show Parker that I have a daddy?"

Olivia's words ripped open Brooke's chest. God, how had she not known?

"Tell me when you want me there," Colin promised.

"Yeah," she said. "Parker can't call me ill-"

First thing tomorrow morning there would be a conversation with Olivia's teacher about this brat Parker.

"So now will you eat some pizza for me?" he asked.

She glanced at the food on her plate. "Can I have a cookie?"

Tears clogged Brooke's throat. Colin glanced at her and seemed to understand.

"Not unless you eat one piece of pizza for me."

"And if I don't?"

"No cookies, no games," Colin said, and Brooke wanted to thank him.

Olivia was testing him.

"Mommy, I don't have to eat my pizza, do I?"

Brooke cleared her throat. "No, you don't have to eat your pizza, but no games or cookies for you tonight."

Olivia frowned, picked up her pizza and took a large

bite. As soon as she had the first bite, she soon followed it with another. And then she ate like a little girl who was hungry.

Brooke glanced at Colin. He smiled like he knew everything was okay. But it wasn't. He'd just broken her trust by telling Olivia the truth. And even though Olivia seemed to have taken the news well, Brooke had asked him to wait.

How would her daughter react when he left the two of them behind and returned to his job?

~

"I thought we agreed we weren't going to tell her," Brooke whispered, the irritation in her voice obvious.

Devon smiled as he watched the couple argue Brooke's living room. Children were a natural conflict tool. Regardless of the age of the child, they caused many arguments between parents. They could pit one parent against the other and start an argument between the adults. Devon watched as Brooke and Colin argued over the fact that he'd told Olivia he was her father. The breakup should happen any moment.

He smiled. He was going to win, and there was nothing Gabriella could do.

"You were the one who said we'd wait. My patience was gone. When she asked about her father, I decided it was time to be honest with her," Colin said. "I told you I would never lie to her."

"Did you ever consider how she's going to feel when you suddenly leave?" She wanted to wait until Colin was on his way out the door or never. Whichever came first.

"Of course. I'll be here as much as possible. And when I can't be here in person, there are telephones."

Brooke rolled her eyes. "She's not going to understand that work comes before her."

"Well, I didn't think she'd understand why I hadn't told her the truth when she kept asking about her father."

"She's a kid. In the next five minute, she would have been back to the puppy."

Silence filled the room as the two glared each other down.

Gabriella shimmered into view wearing a white cheerleading outfit. "Man, they're going at it."

"Yes, a good fight to break them up," Devon said with a smile as the couple continued the argument over who and when Olivia should have been told.

"You haven't won yet."

"It's looking good, though," he said with a smirk.

"Have you ever been in love before?" she asked.

"Not that I can remember. I've been out of the loop for a long time."

"That's obvious. They're having this argument because they're falling in love," Gabriella said confidently.

"No. They're fighting over Olivia, and they're about to break up."

"Then you'll be surprised when he admits he loves her and Olivia and decides to make a life with them."

"Nope, he's going to win the competition and once again he'll choose his job. It's what he's always wanted. Nothing is going to stop him from having enough money until he feels secure," Devon hissed. "Which will be never."

"But that's his lesson to learn. Money doesn't make anyone happy or secure. It's the people in our lives that matter."

Devlin relaxed and smiled. "But the people in his life have always disappointed him. His father, his mother, and even Brooke. So he's not going to choose her."

"His father didn't have a chance. Thanks to your team. His mother wanted to come back to him, again your team.

And now you're going after Colin."

"Hey, I don't call the plays. I just execute them."

"Your playbook really sucks where this family is concerned."

Devon smiled. "Like I said, I'm here to execute the plays. It's Colin's decision how he reacts to them."

Gabriella frowned and turned her attention back to Colin. "I'm here to offer him alternatives. Show him he can choose other ways out of your situations."

"These humans can be stupid about the choices they're offered."

"Yes, but Colin could be a good husband and father. He needs love in his life, and after everything he's been through, he deserves someone special like Brooke. Olivia needs her father." Gabriella said, watching the couple.

"And I still need to make my soul count."

"You know Devon, this is not about you and me."

"Maybe not for you, but it is for me."

Devon looked back at the couple. "Shh! We need to hear this."

Brooke stood with her arms crossed, her dark eyes brooding with disapproval. Colin faced her across the room, a scowl on his face. "You're her mother, and you've been doing this a lot longer than me, but I needed her to know I'm her father. I haven't been here for her."

"This is about what's best for my daughter."

He took a deep breath. "Well, she's not just your daughter any longer. She's my daughter too."

"Of course she is."

"Then why do you always refer to her as *my* daughter?"

"Because you weren't…oh crap!" Brooke said, looking lost. She took a deep breath and released it. All her anger seemed to deflate. "I just want her to be okay with the knowledge of who her father is."

"I do too."

"I don't want to see her hurt."

"I don't either." Colin touched Brooke's arm. "We want the same thing. What's best for Olivia. I hadn't planned on telling her tonight. It just seemed to naturally happen," he said, pulling Brooke into his arms.

At first she resisted, and then she melted into his arms. "Sharing her is a big change for me."

He laughed. "Think about it from my side. I have a five-year-old, and I know nothing about kids."

Brooke smiled at him. "Somehow we've got to help each other make this work."

"Yes," Colin said as his lips came down on hers in a kiss that had Devon sweating.

Gabriella sighed. "Oh, look. They're making up."

"Crap!"

She smiled at Devon. "Gotta fly. I have to catch a cheerleader at the basketball game tonight. So long."

With a shimmer of light, she was gone while Devon continued to watch the couple kiss.

He sighed. So far, Colin McDermott had not acted like he'd expected. Either Gabriella's influence or seeing Brooke and meeting Olivia had affected him and not in a way that helped Devon. But he still had one final trick.

Devon would soon give Colin everything he'd ever wanted.

~

Brooke glanced around the hotel ballroom at her coworkers. Everyone who wasn't on call or working tonight was dressed in their best finery, celebrating the holiday season. Some of their major donors were in attendance along with their children. Olivia stood beside her, dressed in a red velveteen Christmas dress. Colin was across the room talking to a board member.

Her heart rate did a little mambo dance at the sight of

Colin dressed in a black tux that was cut to perfection and made him look more like James Bond than a sales rep. Her James Bond. And she hoped to prove it tonight.

Her father had agreed to pick up Olivia after the children visited Santa. Most children left by nine, and in the past Brooke had always gone home. Tonight she wanted to stay for the dancing, and Colin wanted to schmooze the board members and donors.

But first he had volunteered to play Santa one last time. Brooke smiled at the thought of him agreeing to be Santa again. He'd actually turned into a very good Santa.

"Momma, is Santa here tonight?"

"Yes, baby."

She was quiet for a moment. "He's not going to bring me a puppy is he?"

"Olivia, we've been over this a hundred times. Dogs need a yard. We don't have one."

"But if you and Daddy got married, we could buy a house, and then we could get a dog."

Brooke felt her mouth drop open. She took a deep breath and wondered how to handle this situation. "Honey, why do you think we'll get married?"

Olivia shrugged. "Parker said that parents are supposed to be married."

Brooke wanted to strangle that little brat in day school. He'd caused nothing but trouble.

She knelt down beside her daughter. "Our situation is different from most parents."

"But if you and Daddy got married, we could move out of the apartment and into a house. I could get a puppy and even a baby brother or sister," she said, her emerald eyes excited. "Let's talk to Daddy."

Oh my God, how should she respond? She glanced over at Colin for guidance, but he was gone. Probably slipping into his Santa costume. But what if Olivia asked Santa for her parents to get married, not knowing that her father was Santa?

"Olivia, please let's not discuss this with Santa. Let's keep this to ourselves."

"Why?"

"Colin could move to California soon for his job, and we can't leave here. Ask for a new baby doll or something simple."

Olivia frowned. "I don't want Daddy to move. I don't want a baby doll. I have three already."

"Then ask for a new game. Just don't ask for your daddy and me to get married or for a dog."

She threw her hands in the air. Her bottom lip stuck out, pouting. "Why am I even going to go see him if I can't ask for what I want?"

"Stay here with me," Brooke said, turning her attention away from her daughter in the hopes it would end her tantrum.

Olivia stomped off to get in the line that was forming for Santa, and Brooke wanted to go after her daughter and try to smooth things over. With Olivia being in a snit, there was no telling what she would say.

Just then the president of the hospital board walked up and introduced his wife. All Brooke could do was watch her daughter step up to see Santa.

$\sim$

Colin smiled as his baby girl stepped up to sit on his lap believing he was Santa.

"Olivia, how are you tonight? You look very pretty."

"Thank you."

"I'm supposed to ask you what you want for Christmas, but I already know you want a puppy."

"Nope. My Mom says I can't have one."

Colin frowned. "Okay, so what else do you want for

Christmas?"

She crossed her arms over her chest. "I can't tell you. My mommy says I'm not supposed to ask. I'm supposed to say I want a new baby doll."

"You know we don't always get what we want."

"Duh! I can't have a puppy. I can't have my parents get married so we can all live together. I can't have a house where I can have a dog." Her eyes grew large, and her hand flew to her mouth. "Oops, I wasn't supposed to say that."

"Which part?"

"I never said any of that. Bring me a baby doll."

Before Colin could respond, she jumped down and ran away, leaving him stunned. She wanted her parents together like a family? He'd never experienced real family life with a mother and father who cared. He was trying to learn how to be a father, but a husband?

Wow! That was a thought. He and Brooke married, with Olivia, all living together as a family. With fierceness he didn't understand, he wanted to try. He wanted to be the father he'd never had. He wanted his daughter to experience the love he'd never experienced from his own father.

But more than anything, he wanted Brooke.

But how did he become a father and a husband *and* move to California?

~

Later that evening, after he'd brought Brooke home from the Christmas party, they sat sipping water while a fire burned in the fireplace.

"How was Olivia tonight with Santa?" Brooke asked, afraid of what her daughter had told Colin.

Colin sighed. "She acted a little strange. She said she couldn't ask for what she really wanted and then said just bring her a doll."

Brooke relaxed. Her daughter hadn't spilled her guts to Colin about what she truly wanted, the three of them together as a family.

"She was strange with Santa, yet she came over and kissed me good-bye when your father picked her up," Colin said. "Sometimes she calls me daddy and sometimes she calls me Colin. I think she's still adjusting to the fact that I'm her father."

Brooke smiled. "I know she likes having a father. I never knew what the kids in preschool said to her. I'd like to strangle that little Parker for causing trouble."

Colin sighed. "I wish I'd been here for you both from the beginning."

Brooke heaved a sigh. She felt so guilty for never telling him the truth about Olivia. "You're so good with Olivia. But I still don't understand why you told me that day that you didn't want children. You mentioned lack of control, but how does that relate to not having children? I know you said you didn't have a father. But help me understand."

Colin stood and went to the fireplace. He stirred the wooden logs in the fire and sat down beside her. He stretched his arm along the back of the sofa, bringing her in close to his body. The warmth of him seeped into her side and warmed her heart.

"I only recently learned that my father died the night I was conceived," he said. "I was conceived after the homecoming dance, the same night my father died."

Brooke laid her hand on his arm.

"As if that wasn't bad enough, my eighteen-year-old mother refused the help of my grandparents. She dropped out of high school and had me. I remember we were always moving and she always promised me that things would get better. But she had a problem finding and holding a good paying job. There were times we struggled."

"Is that why you were homeless?"

"Yes."

"How old were you?"

"The first time I remember, I was five. Olivia's age."

"That's why you made certain Olivia had food and shelter."

"Yes." He took a deep breath. "When I was seven everything fell apart. On Christmas Eve my mother took me Christmas shopping and to see Santa. We had a wonderful day together, and I remember being happy. Afterwards, she took my toys and clothes and dropped me off at my grandmother's. That was the last time I ever saw her. She promised to return before Santa came, but she never did."

"Oh my God," Brooke said, her heart going out to the little boy. "It was Christmas. No wonder you hate Christmas. You must have been so hurt waiting for her to return."

His eyes turned dark, and she could see the hate reflecting from their depths. She could almost picture him as a wounded little boy constantly wondering when his mother would return.

"Devastated. I never wanted to have children because I didn't want to risk my children being left with no parents. No one to take care of them."

"This is why you were so concerned about Olivia having a guardian."

"Yes. My grandmother did the best she could, but I wanted my parents. I wanted my mother. And I always wondered about my father."

Brooke thought about Olivia. She'd asked questions about her father and wanted her parents together just like Colin had. Now knowing what was happening in preschool, Brooke felt guilty that she'd never told Olivia about her father.

"I can't say that I wouldn't have pushed you to get rid of the baby all those years ago, but I can't walk away from you and Olivia now. I want her to have the father I never had." He took a deep breath. "And I want to see where our relationship goes. In college I thought we had something special. Something that would last, and then you were gone."

"I'm sorry, Colin. I was so confused. When you said you didn't want children, I freaked out. I ran home to my parents. I let them help me," she said trailing her finger up and down his arm.

She'd been a single mother, just like Colin's mom, and yet she'd had the help of her parents. What a struggle to try to have a baby, do everything on your own without a decent-paying job.

"I never considered you could be pregnant, which makes me feel like an ass. When the condom broke that night, I assumed everything was okay. I'm sorry for being so stupid," he said, pulling her into his arms more tightly.

Brooke laid her head on his shoulder. Suddenly she remembered what Olivia wanted Santa to bring her for Christmas. "Where would we be now if I'd told you the truth all those years ago?"

"I don't know. We were both young. I'd probably have screwed up. I don't know how to be a good father, but I'm willing to learn. Please help me become a good father for our daughter."

Brooke's heart swelled with love for this man. She reached up, cupped his face in her hand and brought his lips down to hers. She gently tasted him. They were alone. No alcohol had been consumed. She wanted him with a hunger she'd not felt since college.

He lowered her onto the couch, his lips persuading her to open her mouth for him as he tasted her thoroughly. His mouth reluctantly left hers. "God, I've missed you."

"No more talking unless you're saying something that turns me on." She smiled at him and pulled his lips back down to hers.

"Tell me what you want me to say besides the fact that I've wanted and missed you for years," he said breathlessly against her lips.

"Hm me too. You don't know how many times those first few months, I almost picked up the phone to call you. I felt so alone."

"I'm here now."

"Yes, you are, and I'm glad."

She pulled his head down until his lips were on hers once again. Her hands slid down his head to his neck, shoulders, and then eased down his back, pressing her body into his. To hold him in her arms was a dream so long denied.

His hands slipped beneath her, lifting her hips to meet his. His erection pressed strong and hard against her. She moaned deep in her throat. She wanted so much more.

He sat up and rubbed his face. "If we go any further, you know how this is going to end."

"How?" she asked with a smile.

"With the two of us naked in your bed."

She sat up. "Let's see, Olivia is at my father's tonight. We neither one have had any alcohol to drink. We're stone cold sober, which is how we promised it would be if we slept together again. I think its decision time."

She stood and looked down at him. "I'm going to bed. You can either join me or go home. Your choice."

He stood, "That's an easy decision."

Chapter Fifteen

Colin followed Brooke to the bedroom, where she lifted her hair off her back. "Would you please unzip me?"

Could he unzip her? Hell, yes!

He slid the zipper down her evening dress, the sound loud in the quiet of the bedroom. She turned to face him, letting the front of her dress fall to expose her bare breasts.

The dress slithered past her waist, past her stomach to land softly on the floor. She stood before him wearing a red silk thong and nothing else.

Hurriedly he unbuttoned his shirt, pulling it from the tux's cummerbund and yanking the shirt out of his pants. He took out his wallet, pulled out the condom he carried, and laid the package on the nightstand. Then he undid the button at his waist, slid his zipper down, and let his pants fall to the floor. He stepped out of the pants. In a matter of seconds, he stood naked before her.

She smiled and stepped into his arms.

"You feel so good," she said, wrapping her arms around him, pressing her breasts into his chest.

Colin thought he was going to die. This moment couldn't be happening. Since they'd met in college, this woman, more than any other, had intrigued him. Had made him nuts, and now once again she was naked in his arms.

When his mouth found hers, he kissed her like she was a lifeline and he was a drowning man. His lips moved over hers hungrily, stroking her until he saw stars from lack of oxygen.

Her naked breasts were crushed against his chest, their fullness warm against his skin. Desire spiraled through him, leaving him longing to kiss those delicious mounds.

He released her lips as he pulled her towards the bed. When she lay down, she pulled the sheet up over her. He joined her under the sheet, which he promptly kicked out of the way. His lips found hers once again while his hand skimmed her satin skin until he touched her breast. He kneaded the pebbled nipple, longing to replace his fingers with his mouth. Gently he broke away, kissing his way across her chest, loving the feel of her body.

She tasted like silk and smelled like roses.

"Oh, Colin," she moaned.

The sound of her passion only made him more intoxicated by her touch.

She combed her fingers through his hair, holding his mouth to her breasts while she wrapped her long legs around his waist, pulling him against her.

Tonight was about them. Not about Olivia, but about the passion they still felt for each other. Even after all these years, he still wanted Brooke.

"Oh no," he said, "not yet."

He kissed his way across her smooth skin, past her waist until he found her center. She gasped as his fingers touched her slick folds. She arched her back and whimpered with delight when he slid his finger inside her.

Throwing her head back, she closed her eyes and moaned with pleasure. He moved down the bed until his mouth was even with her center and licked her slippery folds.

"Colin," she cried.

He kissed her intimately, expressing his love the only way he could by making certain she reached the highest of heights. He loved hearing her express her passion, knowing he'd brought her pleasure.

He licked her womanly center as she clutched the hair on the top of his head. Holding off his own release, he was determined to make certain that her pleasure came before his. Tonight he needed her like a dying man's last breath. He wanted her. Had longed for her, for so many years.

No other woman had ever interested him the way

Brooke had, and being together tonight seemed right. He felt like he'd come home, where he belonged.

In no time, she was clutching his head, holding onto him as spasms rocked her body. She cried out, "Colin."

As soon as the last spasm died away, he reached over to the nightstand and found the condom he'd pulled from his pocket earlier. In seconds he'd ripped open the foil packet and rolled the glove over his erection.

He slid his body up hers and plunged into her, relishing the feel of her body accepting him. She gasped with pleasure as her body wrapped around him, squeezing him. He tried to go slow, to let her catch up with him, but the rasp of her breathing and the way her body met his, equally giving and taking with each thrust, was too much.

Though he wanted this time to last forever, he'd never thought this would happen between them again. She felt like heaven, and he tried to make it last. For her, for him, but with each stroke, he knew he was racing to the edge. The need to pound into her was overwhelming.

Only with Brooke did he feel this need to claim her as his. To show her that she was the only woman in his life and to demonstrate his love for her. In this moment nothing mattered but Brooke.

The thought stunned him.

The realization he was falling in love with her all over again sent him tumbling over the edge. Like a cliff jumper, he went sailing over a bright expanse with Brooke as his parachute.

Her nails dug into his back as her body spasmed with pleasure, clinging to Colin, rescuing him as he landed on soft ground once again.

Slowly he recovered in her arms, holding her sated body against his. He loved Brooke.

When had that happened? College? Hell, he couldn't remember *not* being in love with her.

What in the hell did he do now? Run like the hounds of hell were after him, or cave in to his feelings and stay here in Crystal Mountain?

~

Brooke arrived at her father's the next morning to pick up Olivia. Walking through the door, she heard her daughter and father laughing.

As she entered the den, she watched the two of them together watching *Miracle on 34th Street*. When Olivia saw her, she jumped up and ran to Brooke, throwing her arms around her legs.

"Hi, Mom," she said, still in her pajamas.

"Hi, sweetness. Did you have a good time?"

"Oh, yes," she said. "This little girl in the movie gets her wish. Her parents get married and buy a house. I bet she even gets a dog."

"It's a movie, Olivia. It's not reality."

Her daughter moved away from her and sank onto the floor in front of the television, obviously not pleased with her response.

Her dad rose from the couch. "Sorry, we've been couch potatoes this morning. Olivia wanted to watch the movie again before she went home."

"That's all right."

"Would you like some coffee?" her father asked.

"That sounds wonderful."

Several minutes later, she and her father were sitting across from each other at the kitchen table. An overwhelming sense of loss hit her as she sat in what was once her mother's kitchen. She missed her so much.

"Where's Colin this morning?"

"He donates one Saturday a month at a homeless shelter. This is his Saturday."

"That's nice."

"Yeah, it is," she said, remembering the way they'd said good-bye this morning. How she hadn't wanted him to leave.

"How's it going with you two?" he asked.

She bit her lip and looked at her coffee. "It's going so well that I'm scared."

Her father smiled. "Just go slow, and don't let little missy rush you into a decision you'll regret."

"Yeah, I know. We have so much baggage between us. Dad, how can he ever forgive me for not telling him about Olivia? If our positions were reversed, I'd hate him. I was wrong, Dad. I should have told him I was pregnant."

"You were young. You were frightened. You didn't even tell us who the father was," he said, listing the very real reasons behind her actions.

"But we made Olivia together. I didn't give him the opportunity to choose whether or not he wanted to be her father," she said, taking a sip of coffee to try to keep the tears at bay.

Her father shook his head and stared into her eyes. "No, but he's been given that chance now."

"Yes. Without my permission he told Olivia that he was her father. Yet I can't blame him. I don't know when I would have let him tell her," she admitted.

"You're her mother, and you're protective of her. She seems happy to know she has a father. I worry that if he leaves, she'll be disappointed."

"Me, too. If he wins that promotion, he'll be moving to California."

"Do you think he would ask you and Olivia to go with him?"

Brooke thought for a moment. "The bigger problem is that I'm not willing to uproot Olivia and leave my job behind, nor you, on the chance that we might make it as a couple. Until I'm certain that this relationship is good for me and Olivia, I can't uproot our lives to follow him to California."

"Even if you love him?"
"I'm scared, Dad. I think I'm falling in love with him, but I can't risk him running out on me and Olivia. That would devastate both of us. I have to think about Olivia's welfare."

"Honey, you always think of her welfare. But what about you? You say you're falling in love with him. Give the man a chance. If he asks you to go to California, don't automatically say no. Give it some consideration."

"But Dad, I'd be leaving you."

"The road goes both ways, and there are planes, trains and automobiles. I'd miss both of you, but your happiness is what's important."

For a moment Brooke considered what her father had said. "I just don't know if he's forgiven me for not telling him about Olivia."

"You need to settle that before you go much further. I think you should ask for his forgiveness."

She shook her head, not looking forward to that conversation, especially after spending the night in his arms. A night that was even better than the night Olivia was conceived.

"You're right. It's a conversation that we've both avoided. I need to ask him."

~

Later that afternoon Brooke followed Colin into the senior citizens care facility.

"Are you certain this is a good idea?" Brooke asked, uneasy about walking into the nursing home.

"Yes, Grammy wants to meet the two of you. She's very excited you're coming today," Colin said as they walked through the doors.

Olivia glanced up at her mother. "It smells funny in here."

"Yes, it does, but don't mention it," Brooke told her daughter.

The three of them walked down the hall, Brooke and Colin holding Olivia's hands between them. They passed open doors with elderly patients sitting in their chairs staring at the television. Some waved as they passed. Some just stared into space, oblivious to their surroundings.

A speaker announced that bingo would start in thirty minutes.

Brooke felt uncertain. After everything she'd learned of Colin's past, she knew his grandmother was his only living relative that he knew of and how much he loved her. To bring them to meet his grandmother was an enormous step for him.

They reached her door. Colin released Olivia's hand and went in first. Brooke and Olivia followed behind him.

A wiry, short lady with gray hair and warm eyes stood and wrapped her arms around Colin.

"Colin, it's so good to see you," she said.

"Merry Christmas, Grammy. I brought Brooke and Olivia to meet you," he said, stepping out of her arms.

"So this is your family?" his grandmother said.

Brooke glanced at Colin, not certain how to react to that statement.

His grandmother shuffled toward Brooke. "It's so good to meet you," she said, wrapping her arms around Brooke to give her a brief hug.

Colin shook his head at Brooke. "Grammy, you said you wanted to meet Olivia."

"Oh, yes," she said, bending to look at her great-granddaughter. She didn't try to hug her, but just peered at her with a smile on her face.

"I'm your great-grandmother," she said. "I'm your

father's grandmother."

"Hi," Olivia said, seeming a little uncertain. She glanced around the room and then up at Colin. "Where's your mommy?"

Brooke's heart sank. She should have told her before they left this morning. She glanced at Colin, seeing the sadness reflected in his eyes. His mouth was tense as if he struggled with an answer.

There was a moment of silence before Colin said, "I don't know what happened to my mommy. I haven't seen her since I was a little boy. I think she must be dead."

Brooke blinked back tears as she watched the emotion in his face and knew how hard it was for him to admit his mother was dead. To answer questions about his past was big. To tell Olivia about his mother was even bigger.

His grandmother patted him on the arm. "Let me show you a picture of Colin's mother, your grandmother. She was a beautiful young woman. You favor her."

Olivia looked at her mother and then back to Colin's grandmother. "Okay."

The elderly woman picked up a photo album that lay nearby and caressed the cover. She gazed at Colin. "Since you came to visit me the other day, I haven't had the heart to put the pictures away. I've looked at them every day."

Colin nodded, and she opened the album. Brooke stared in shock at the pictures of Colin's mother as a child. She bore a striking resemblance to Olivia.

As the three of them looked at the photos in the album, Brooke glanced at Colin. He seemed more at peace than she'd ever seen him, and she wondered at the difference just a couple of weeks had made.

Had he finally accepted that his mother was never returning?

His grandmother's hand reached out and took hold of hers. "I'm so happy that Colin has you and Olivia. Seeing the three of you together has made me so happy." She ruffled Olivia's hair. "And you little lady, I'm so glad to meet you."

"Me, too," Olivia said. "Now I have a grandpa and a grandma."

"Why don't you call me Grammy," his grandmother said.

"Okay, Grammy."

"We've got to leave," Colin said. "But I wanted to bring them by before the holidays. I needed you to meet my daughter."

Tears welled in the older woman's eyes. "Thank you, Colin. You've made me very happy."

Colin hugged his grandmother good-bye, and they walked out of the room. Brooke saw tears shimmer in his eyes, and she knew he was remembering his mother. Only now she saw tenderness instead of hate.

~

Colin's cell phone rang. He'd just finished his last appointment for the week. Three days from now they would announce the promotion, and he'd only sold two clients. He could blame it on the time of year, or he could admit his heart just hadn't been in the game this time.

"Hello."

"Olivia is in bed. Do you want to come over?"

He smiled. "I'm on my way."

Ten minutes later, he quietly knocked on her door.

Brooke opened the door, and he pulled her into his arms for a kiss. When he held her, it felt like she belonged in his arms and winning no longer mattered. Sure he'd worked all year for this promotion, but nothing mattered when Brooke's lips were on his.

She broke the kiss, leaning back to smile at him. "That was quite a hello."

"I missed you."

"It's been less than ten hours since you've seen me."

"Much too long."

She laughed. "Come in."

She took his coat and hung it up. "Olivia went down early tonight. She wanted to watch *Miracle on 34th Street*, again."

"Good show."

"But not realistic."

"Sometimes fantasy is a good thing."

"Maybe."

He settled onto the couch and patted the seat beside him.

"We've got to talk," she said. A worried frown creased her forehead.

"Okay."

She stood and paced the room. "I know that we've been kind of playing dodgeball about this whole situation with Olivia."

"What do you mean? I'm involved in her life. I've arranged for child support."

Brooke stopped in front of him and shifted uncomfortably. "You've been more than generous to me and to her." She clasped her hands and sank into a chair across from him. "I don't know how else to say this."

She took a deep breath and released it. "I want to apologize to you for not telling you the truth about the pregnancy. I have no other excuse than to say I was young and frightened and didn't know what to do. Please forgive me for keeping you away from your daughter. I've realized I made a huge mistake, and I'm sorry."

Colin absorbed the fact she was apologizing. He hadn't wanted to be a father, and he was afraid to think about the decision he would have made if she'd given him a chance. That little girl lying in bed might not be here if he'd been involved. Or maybe he and Brook would have married and had a second child by now. Or maybe nothing would have been different. He didn't know. As much as he appreciated Brooke's apology, they had to move on.

Colin frowned. "Brooke, I was young and stupid too. I don't know what my reaction would have been at the time, and I'm afraid it wouldn't have been my finest moment. We have a beautiful, bright kid, and I'm glad for the opportunity to get to know her now. Sure I wish I'd been here when she was born, but maybe it was for the best I wasn't."

"You don't hate me for not telling you?"

He shrugged. "I was angry when I first learned about Olivia. But I want to put this behind us and concentrate on the future. Let's agree to always work together for what's best for Olivia."

Brooke sighed. "Thank you, Colin."

"Now are you going to cuddle with me or not?" he asked.

She smiled and came to sit beside him. "Cuddling is about the only thing we can do."

"When does your father want to babysit again?"

She laughed. "I'll ask him to watch her one night this weekend."

"That's too long. And…" he stopped. This weekend the contest would be over, and he would either be on a plane to California or still here in Crystal Mountain.

"What's wrong?" Brooke asked.

He sighed. "I could be on a plane to California this weekend."

Brooke frowned. "The board is due to make their decision day after tomorrow."

"Oh," he said.

For a moment, silence filled the room as he thought about how far they'd come in the last few weeks. How his focus had gone from being the top-rated salesperson to being Santa Claus, to being a father.

What in the hell would he do if he won the promotion?

Brooke snuggled into his side. "Would you mind watching Olivia for me tomorrow afternoon? I need to get stocking stuffers, and then we're ready for Santa."

"Sure," he said, still wondering if he wanted to leave Brooke and Olivia. "What time?"
"It shouldn't take long. Why don't you come over about four and I'll fix chili afterwards."

"I'll be here," he said, wanting to spend as much time with his girls as he could just in case he won the promotion. But winning wasn't looking so good. After all, he'd only sold two packages. Even if Crystal Mountain General, Brooke's hospital, came through, he still thought Logan had sold more units.

But the crucial question was did he still want this promotion?

~

Colin watched as Brooke backed out of her parking space and turned to see Olivia staring at him.

"What do you want to do while Mommy's gone?" he asked.

An impish smile lit her face. "I want to build a snowman."

Colin frowned. "Aren't you tired of the snow yet? This is like the third or fourth snowstorm we've had."

"Nope. Let's go build a snowman."

He glanced at her. "Okay, but you have to put on your snowsuit, including ear muffs."

"I don't like ear muffs."

"Then we're not going outside."

"I don't know where they are."

"Then we're not going outside."

She frowned at him and went into her room. Colin sat on the sofa, relieved he'd won that skirmish and they were going to stay inside.

The snow had stopped falling, but a north wind blew, and the temperature hovered around twenty-five degrees. Not exactly prime snowman-building weather.

The door to Olivia's room opened, and she stepped out in her snowsuit with her earmuffs and mittens on. "Let's go."

Crap. She'd found her earmuffs.

"I thought you didn't know where your earmuffs were."

"They were with my snowsuit."

"I see that."

"Don't forget the carrot. We need a carrot for his nose," she told him.

Colin slipped on his ski jacket and went to the refrigerator for the carrot, not really looking forward to being in the cold.

"You'll tell me if you start getting cold?"

"Uh-huh," she said.

"You don't want to be sick over Christmas."

She shook her head no. "Huh-uh."

"Okay, let's go get this snowman built and get back inside where it's warm," he said, opening the door.

They stepped outside the apartment and the wind hit Colin square in the chest, sending a shock through his system. "Let's make this quick."

"Show me how."

He stopped and contemplated her. Was she spoofing him? "You've never built a snowman before?"

She shook her head. "No."

He frowned, wondering why Brooke had never made a snowman with Olivia. He reached down in the snow and made a snowball. "You start with a packed snowball. Then you place it in the snow and start to roll your snowball.

You pack as much snow as possible onto the smaller ball and keep rolling.”

Olivia watched him. Finally, the ball became large enough that the two of them could roll the snowball.

When the ball was large enough for a base, they stopped. “Okay, now we do it again. You do it this time.”

She packed a snowball and then laid it in the snow. It didn’t roll. She picked the snowball up and threw it at Colin.

It hit him square in the chest.

“Hey!”

She giggled. “Oops, it fell out of my hand.”

“Yeah, right.”

Colin came over and helped her get the snowball rolling. Soon they had a ball for the middle section of the snowman. On the third ball, Olivia pretty much did it by herself, and when the ball was large enough, she handed it to Colin.

He placed it on the top of the other two packed snowballs.

“Yippee! We have a snowman!”

“Find me a couple of rocks for his eyes and mouth,” Colin said, looking for sticks for the arms.

A few minutes later, Olivia ran back to him with her gloves full of small rocks. “Here. We can use these for his eyes and mouth.”

They placed the items on the snowman, along with the carrot from the house, and then stood back to admire their handiwork. “Not too bad for a first snowman.”

“I can’t wait for Mommy to see.”

“Have you ever made snow angels?”

Olivia’s eyes grew wide, and she shook her head. “No. Are they like snowmen?”

“I’ll show you.” Colin laid down in the snow. He moved his arms and legs until it formed the skirt and wings of the angel.

Olivia dropped into the snow and followed his example. When Colin stood, snow covered his backside.

Olivia giggled at him. "You're snowy."

Just then Brooke drove up in the car.

"*Uh oh*," Olivia said, seeing her Mom getting out of the car.

The frosty look on Brooke's face suddenly explained to Colin why Olivia had never built a snowman before.

"The wind chill is in the teens. What are you two doing out here?" she asked.

"Look at my snowman, mommy. Isn't he cute?" Olivia said, clearly trying to divert Brooke's attention.

"Didn't I tell you this morning that you couldn't play outside? Now, get in the house before you catch a cold."

"But we're making snow angels."

"You're both covered in snow. In the house," she commanded.

Olivia started toward the house. Colin took the bag of groceries from Brooke's arms.

"Did you ever consider that after having surgery her immune system is weak? Did you think that she could catch cold or pneumonia?" Brook asked, clearly frustrated.

"She wanted to go outside. I thought I was doing well by making her put her earmuffs on."

"She's a child, Colin. You're the parent. Tell her no."

"Hey, I'm still learning this parenting game."

Brooke turned and glared at him. "No joke. She just manipulated you big time, because I told her this morning she couldn't go out and build a snowman."

"Oh," he said feeling a little foolish at how his daughter had maneuvered him. He'd been outwitted by a five-year-old. "Maybe you're being a little overprotective," he said.

"Maybe I am. But two weeks ago she had to have surgery. Excuse me for being overprotective."

They reached the door and stopped. Olivia stood watching the two of them, her eyes sad and her mouth drawn in a pout.

"Maybe I should go," Colin said.

Brooke took a deep breath and sighed. "No. We're all still adjusting. Let's get her inside and put her in a warm bath."

"Mommy, Colin wasn't going to hurt me," Olivia said.

"Olivia, you know you can't play in the snow right now."

"But I wanted to."

"Get inside and into the bathtub."

"You won't send Daddy home, will you?"

"No, I won't send him home."

"Okay," she said and ran into the house.

Brooke turned to Colin.

"Give me a break. I'm still learning. And she took full advantage of my lack of parenting skills," he said.

Brooke smiled. "She knows how to play you."

"Yes, she does. I'm a sucker when she turns on the charm. I'm at a disadvantage here."

"Yes, you are. Now you can prepare the chili while I give her a bath," Brooke said.

Colin kissed her lightly on the lips. "You're not mad at me any longer?"

"No, I feel sorry for you. You are in so much trouble with this child."

They walked in the house together, and Colin shook his head. "Yes, I know. And her mother has me wrapped around her little finger too. I'm in big trouble with both of you."

Chapter Sixteen

Brooke sat staring at the phone, knowing she should call Colin, but not wanting to deliver the news. The hospital board had unanimously decided to purchase his software. While it was advantageous for Colin, she feared what this would do for them as a family. But were they a family?

Today was the final day of the contest. If she waited just one more day, it would mean he couldn't count her hospital. It could possibly keep him from winning the sales director's position.

But was that fair? Even with her hospital's sale, he could still lose the contest. His competitor might have outsold him. Her thoughts were selfish. She knew they were, but the thought of him leaving was devastating. Still, if he found out she'd kept the truth from him, then whatever trust they'd managed to create would be gone.

No matter what happened, whether he stayed or went to California, this had to be Colin's decision. If he won, he would have to choose between staying with Brooke and Olivia or taking the promotion.

She was through keeping secrets from him. This time they would deal with whatever decision he made together. Like they should have when she'd learned she was pregnant.

He might ask them to join him in California, but she knew she couldn't uproot Olivia, quit her job, and follow him blindly with only the chance that they'd eventually marry.

This promotion wasn't a certainty, but whatever happened, she had to let Colin choose his path.

She picked up the phone and punched in his number.

"Hi," she said, forcing cheerfulness into her voice.

"Hi," he responded. "What was the decision?"

He'd obviously been waiting for her call. "I have all the signed documents here on my desk. You just need to pick them up."

"Yes!" he said into the phone. "I'll come by before lunch. All paperwork has to be in by two o'clock this afternoon."

"Good luck," she said, trying to force some enthusiasm into her voice, knowing what a win for Colin would do to their fragile relationship.

"If I win, we're going out to celebrate."

"When will you find out?" she asked, certain her stomach would be tied up like a contortionist, until the contest ended and the winner was announced.

"Tomorrow. And then the winner flies out on Christmas Eve."

"Christmas Eve," she said in horror. "Why so soon? Seems you could wait until after Christmas."

"No, they want the new director there December twenty-six, ready to start work immediately," he said.

Silence stretched on the phone. Brooke had known he would have to leave soon, but she hadn't expected him to leave before Christmas.

"You'll miss Christmas with Olivia," she said.

"And you," he said softly into the phone. "We don't know for certain that I'm going to win the position. Logan has had steady sales."

That was true, but somehow it didn't make her feel any better. "I've got to run. I have a meeting in five minutes. The paperwork is with Cynthia, my secretary, if I'm not here."

"Brooke, we'll work this out whatever happens," he promised.

She didn't say anything. She feared if he left their chance of them being a couple was over. How could a long-distance relationship between two people who were both career oriented work? Just like him, she had dreams. She wanted to stay here at this hospital and become the chief administrator.

"See you tonight," she said, disconnecting the call. She wasn't going to lie to him and say that she hoped he won this promotion. Frankly, she hoped he didn't.

~

Colin sat with Logan in Ed's office once again. They'd come full circle and were where it all began four weeks ago, about to learn the results of the contest.

He had no idea if he'd won. And somehow he wasn't as anxious as before. Sure he still wanted the promotion, but it wasn't as -consuming. Now there was Olivia to consider, but most of all Brooke. Could he leave behind the woman who'd always intrigued him? Who he'd wanted since college?

Ed was speaking, and Colin was too busy contemplating what he would lose if he won this position.

"You guys once again proved that you're great salesmen. We're lucky to have you both. I feel confident the loser will someday be one of our regional directors. It's just a matter of time." He took a deep breath. "Our new western sales director is…Colin McDermott."

Stunned, Colin didn't move as shock coursed through his veins. He hadn't thought he would win. He thought Logan had more sales.

Part of him was jumping up and down inside while the other part smiled but knew the sacrifices were going to hurt. Now he would have the million-dollar salary with the big bonus. Everything he'd ever wanted was within his grasp, yet he had mixed emotions, and he hadn't expected both the joy and the sadness.

"Congratulations," Logan said, holding out his hand. "You'll do an excellent job."

Colin shook his hand. "Thank you. You're a strong competitor."

Ed opened his desk drawer and pulled out an envelope, handing it to Colin. "Here is your plane ticket for Christmas Eve. That gives you Christmas Day to set up your office and hit the ground running the day after Christmas."

"Is there any way that I can leave Christmas Day?"

"Sorry, we want to make certain you're there for the day after Christmas."

He nodded. "Okay, well thanks for everything. I can't wait to get started."

His boss smiled at him. "You were meant for this position, Colin."

Colin couldn't restrain the grin. He'd beat Logan and secured the position. "Thanks."

He walked out the door to the office. He'd achieved his goal. He was now western sales director. His salary had tripled. He would now be one of the top five in the company.

So why didn't he feel more excited and happy? Why did Brooke's face keep appearing in his mind, reminding him of what he'd miss?

~

Devon smiled and watched as Gabriella shimmered into appearance.

"This time *you* lose. He accepted the position."

"It's not over until the fat lady sings, and I haven't heard her belting out a song just yet."

Devon smiled and looked over her opera outfit. "Too bad you don't have some weight on you, or you could be the fat lady."

She twisted her mouth in a frown. "I don't think so."

"I guess you'd better be prepared to comfort Olivia and Brooke. His flight leaves at six-thirty on Christmas Eve.

"I wouldn't count his soul until he steps on that plane."

"Oh, I'm not worried. The bonus round is about to begin, and I have a little something extra planned to guarantee he'll be on that plane."

"Devon, this is the absolute meanest I have ever seen you play."

"I need this win. Make quota or spend time in the pit."

"I'm not giving up," Gabriella said with a shake of her long, blonde hair. "Like I said, I don't hear the fat lady singing just yet. I don't give up on a soul until it's too late, and there's nothing else to be done."

"I know. But Colin McDermott is mine."

~

Brooke sat in her office, staring out the window at the snow-covered parking lot below.

Colin had called just a few minutes ago to say that her hospital's purchase had won him the position. He was now the new western sales director and he'd be leaving Christmas Eve to travel to the west coast.

Christmas Eve. Why couldn't they wait until Christmas Day to say good-bye? How was she going to explain to Olivia that Daddy no longer lived here and wouldn't be spending Christmas with them?

Who was she kidding? It wasn't just about Olivia. She was upset because he was leaving.

Amelia stuck her head in the doorway. "Santa arrived early."

"What? I thought we were done with Santa visits."

"We are. But Emma and her mother just received a package from Santa. It seems Emma asked Santa to bring her mother a new blue dress, because she never bought herself anything new. Three new dresses were just delivered along with one for the little girl."

"Who delivered them?"

"The store. But our own Santa, aka Colin, purchased them."

Brooke understood what Colin had done for the little girl. For a man who hated Christmas, the Santa suit seemed to have changed him. But not enough to help him realize what he was leaving behind with the new promotion.

"Who died?" Amelia asked.

"What do you mean?"

"You're sitting here staring into space with a look of utter despair on your face instead of being happy that Santa helped someone beside himself."

"Colin won the promotion."

"Great! Tell him I said congratulations."

Brooke gazed at her friend, all the pain she'd kept inside exposed in her eyes.

"Oh, so that's how it is. You don't want him to leave," Amelia said. "Wow. I never thought I'd see this day."

Brooke laid her head down on her desk. "I never thought I would feel this way about him again. What do I do now? I love him, and he's leaving."

"Maybe he'll ask you to go with him."

"And what am I supposed to do? Yank Olivia out of preschool, give up my job and follow him?"

Amelia nodded her head. "Yeah, I think so. Look, this man may not have started out with a heart of gold, but right now he's at the top of my men-with-good-hearts-chart. You better snatch him up quick."

"That's only because he did the Santa gig for you and gave dresses away to a needy mom."

"A good man comes along, and you're too blind to see that you were meant to be together. Follow him to California."

"I can't go to California after only four weeks of getting to know him again. My daughter needs stability in her life."

"She also needs her father."

"She didn't even know she had a father until two weeks ago," Brooke said, unable to believe the time had passed so quickly.

"Yes, but now she does. Don't make this a situation where she only sees her father on holidays and birthdays. I've lived that kind of life, and it's not good."

Brooke bit her bottom lip. "I just wish we had more time for me to make a decision." She threw up her arms. "Who am I kidding? He hasn't asked me to go with him. I doubt that he wants us to follow him there."

"You guys looked pretty tight the other night at the Christmas party."

"Oh Amelia, you have no idea."

"Oh dear. You gave up the alcohol."

"Yes." She glanced at her friend, squeezing her eyes to keep the tears from overflowing. "This is going to hurt, isn't it? What am I going to do?"

~

Brooke sat across from Colin wearing a fake smile, trying to celebrate his success and knowing she was failing miserably. Her father had agreed to keep Olivia for the evening while she and Colin celebrated his promotion.

He leaned forward, taking her hand. "Brooke, this doesn't mean it's over between us."

At first she didn't say anything, just sipped her glass of wine, trying to act happy.

"Once everything is running smoothly, I'll fly you and Olivia out to visit."

"Olivia is in school. She can't miss."

"It will probably be spring break before I could spend some time with you anyway. In the meantime, we'll speak every day."

Brooke wanted to cry but held the tears at bay. "I know, but long distance relationships are so hard. You'll be busy setting up your division, and you'll soon forget us."

"No. I want this to work for both of us."

"Colin, how can it? We've been seeing each for four weeks, and now suddenly you're leaving? I don't know if we have a strong enough foundation to support a long-distance relationship."

He picked up her hand, his brown eyes were warm, his expression genuine. "I know that Olivia's what brought us back together and that we have a past, but I want this to continue. You've always been the girl that got away. And this time I don't want you to slip away again."

Brooke smiled, but her mouth felt stiff. "I'm happy that you've gotten your promotion. I'll give the long-distance thing a chance, but if I think we're fading, then I'm going to end it between us. Even if that happens, I want you to continue to see Olivia. She's been so happy these last few weeks. Please don't disappear from her life."

"Never. But I want to be in your life as well. Before there was Olivia, there was us."

She tried to feel happy, but after tonight, three months would pass before they saw each other again and that depressed the hell out of her.

"I bought you something," Colin said.

He pulled out a small jeweler's box and laid it on the table.

Her breath caught in her throat. No, it was way too early for an engagement ring. She glanced up at him, and he smiled. It couldn't be. Oh God, it just couldn't be. It was too soon. They'd only reconnected the last four weeks.

"Well, aren't you going to open it?"

With trembling fingers, she tore at the ribbon around the box and lifted the lid. Inside was a ring—not an engagement ring-but a mother's ring.

She glanced at him, trying to keep the disappointment off her face, not understanding why he'd chosen this ring. Confusion wracked her and she realized how disappointed she felt that it wasn't an engagement ring. But she should feel relieved, shouldn't she?

"I didn't think it was the right time to give you an engagement ring. We're too old for promise rings, but I thought maybe a mother's ring to signify that I recognize that you're the mother of my child. This is my promise to you to continue our relationship."

Brooke blinked her eyes, trying to keep the tears at bay as she stared down at the ring. Her emotions scattered like the break of pool balls on a table. Her rational self knew it was too early to think of engagements, but the emotional part of her hoped for one just the same. Yet he was promising himself to her and Olivia. But a mother's ring? Crap, why did it just feel wrong? It felt old and about as sexy as flannel pajamas.

He took her hand again. "I want to do right by you and Olivia. I want there to be an 'us'. A family. But I need this time."

She closed her eyes for a moment, trying to understand and give him what he needed. She pushed her disappointment aside. The months apart would show Brooke if Colin was truly committed to them.

"Okay."

"Do you understand?"

"I'm trying."

"What can I do to make it easier?"

"Nothing. Time will tell."

Brooke waited, hoping at least he'd say some words of love. Something. But Colin didn't say anything. Was she the only one whose heart was once again involved and silently breaking?

Her cell phone rang. She picked it up. "Hi, Dad."

"I think you better come home."

"What? Why? What's wrong?" she said, suddenly frightened. Her father never called her to come get Olivia.

"Olivia's throwing up. I took her temperature a few minutes ago, and she's running a hundred and two," her father answered. "I thought I better let you know."

"I'm on my way. We're leaving now." She ended the call.

"What's wrong?" Colin asked.

"Olivia's sick. I've got to go."

Colin threw money onto the table, and they rushed out of the restaurant.

Brooke worried all the way to her father's. Olivia had never been a sickly child, but her immune system was weak. Was this just a bug or something more serious? A complication from the accident three weeks ago that had gone undiagnosed until now?

"She's a tough little girl. She's going to be okay. It's probably just a cold," Colin said.

"You should never have taken her outside. Now she's ill. If you're going to be her father, you need to think of her safety," Brooke said, all the frustration and fear spilling out into the open.

Irrational anger at Colin, at life, and even at Olivia consumed her. She hated the promotion, the ring he'd given her, but most of all that he was leaving without saying he loved her.

"I do think of her safety. I don't want her to ever experience what I did when my mother disappeared. I want her childhood easy compared to mine," Colin responded as he drove like a maniac through the darkened streets in the snow.

"Then put her welfare before your own. Think about whether or not what you're doing is good for her next time."

"I did, Brooke. But when she told me she'd never made a snowman, I realized she's been coddled way too much," he said, his voice rising.

"She just had surgery, so excuse me for being a mite overprotective." She gripped her purse handles in her hands.

"But what about before? Why had my daughter never made a snowman? Why did she know nothing about snow angels?"

"Oh, please. She's built snowmen before. She played you and you fell for it."

A tense silence filled the car as they stopped in front of her dad's. "Wait for me here."

"No, she's my daughter too. Don't shut me out, Brooke," Colin said, opening the car door.

She glared at him then jumped out of the car and ran up the steps to the front door.

Colin followed more slowly, but caught up to her as she entered the house.

Brooke saw her father sitting in the chair with Olivia in his lap.

"Hi, Hon, she's not doing any better," he said, glancing between the two of them.

"Hi, sweetie. What's wrong?" Brooke asked, kneeling beside Olivia.

"My throat and tummy hurt."

"Why don't we take you home? I'll give you some baby aspirin and put you to bed."

Her father shook his head. "I think you need to take her to the emergency room. I just checked her fever, and it's one hundred and three."

Brooke gasped. "Where's her coat?"

"On the couch."

Together, they managed to get the coat slipped on with both of them putting her arms in. Olivia slid off her grandfather's lap.

Colin picked Olivia up and carried her to the car, not saying anything to Brooke or her father. Brooke climbed into the backseat and he gently laid Olivia in her lap. He pulled the seat belt around them.

"The ER?" he asked.

"Yes," she said.

They drove in silence, yet he could hear Olivia wheezing in the back. With each breath, his heart broke. This is what he'd done to his daughter.

When they pulled up to the emergency room entrance, Colin stopped the car and a nurse came out with a wheelchair. He lifted Olivia and put her in the chair.

"Don't go, Daddy," she said.

The word "Daddy" tore at him. He wasn't a good father. He didn't deserve to be called Daddy. He'd only hurt her since he'd come into her life.

"I'm going to park the car, and then I'll be here."

She started to cry.

"I promise," he said. "Don't cry. It will only make you feel worse."

She sniffled. "Okay."

Brooke glared at him and went into the emergency room with the nurse pushing Olivia.

Crap! Maybe Brooke was right. Maybe he was a terrible father, and he had harmed his daughter by taking her out to play in the snow.

Maybe he'd be doing them both a favor if he just disappeared from their life.

Colin parked the car and walked into the building to find them. The nurse directed him toward Olivia's room. At the door, he heard the doctor.

"Her lungs sound congested. It's either bronchitis or pneumonia. I want to take an X-ray to make certain it's not pneumonia. Let's get some blood work and a chest X-ray."

Pneumonia. It was his fault. He'd harmed his own daughter. The urge to run, to go away where he couldn't make things worse, overwhelmed him.

Brooke was already angry with him. So far, his being involved in Olivia's life had caused more harm than good. She was in Brooke's very capable hands. They were doing quite well on their own before he came into their lives. He needed to leave them alone before he did irreparable damage.

And he certainly didn't need this crap in his life. Sick kid. A woman who was upset that he had gotten the promotion and was moving. She knew his career was important. All this drama distracted him from his goal of making a million dollars, and that goal was within his grasp now.

He had packing to do. He had a plane to catch and a big move to make. If he was such a lousy father, he should leave and let Brooke take care of his daughter. After all, she'd been doing a terrific job of it before he came back into her life.

Colin opened the door and went inside the exam room. Brooke glared at him, and Olivia lay limply on the examining table until they tried to take blood.

Brooke held her in her arms while the nurse stuck the needle in her vein. Olivia screamed. The sound felt like claws ripping his insides to shreds as he watched the pain his daughter experienced and knew it was his fault.

Tears filled Brooke's eyes and he knew seeing Olivia in pain and realizing there was nothing she could do hurt her as well. He'd hurt both of them by his inadequacies as a father.

More than ever he longed to disappear into the night.

Suddenly he felt certain he was doing the right thing by leaving them tomorrow. They were better off without him. Quietly, he slipped out the door.

Chapter Seventeen

Brooke watched as the doctor returned to the room where Olivia lay dozing. They'd given her something for her fever, and already her temperature was dropping.

"Good news. The X-rays came back normal. It's not pneumonia. She probably caught something from one of the kids in day care. I'm writing you a prescription for antibiotics. Take her home, put her in bed, and keep her there for twenty-four hours. She should start to feel better after that. If not, bring her back. But I think it's just a bad cold."

Relief settled over Brooke like a warm blanket. Her daughter was okay. Nothing from the accident. Just a cold. She needed to let Colin know.

She stepped outside to the waiting room where he'd gone once Olivia had settled down. The guilt she'd seen on his face as he watched them draw blood from his daughter had been heart wrenching. He sat slumped in a chair. "She's okay."

He glanced up at her, his eyes dark with some unreadable emotion. "Good."

"Let's get her home," Brooke said. "I have to sign the release papers, and then we can go."

He nodded but didn't say anything.

Ten minutes later, Brooke watched as Colin carried a sleeping Olivia to the car, laid her in the backseat. On the drive home, a tense silence enveloped the car.

Tomorrow was Christmas Eve, and he would be leaving.

Colin carried Olivia into the house, taking her straight to her bed. Brooke undressed her daughter and pulled the covers up tight around her. At the door, she glanced back at the sleeping child and a surge of protective love overwhelmed her. She wouldn't let anything harm her daughter, not even Colin.

When she walked into the living room, Colin was there, pacing the floor.

His eyes were bleak and Brooke realized she'd been hard on him.

"Is she okay?"

"Yes, whatever they gave her lowered her temperature and made her sleepy. She's sound asleep."
He hesitated a moment, shoving his hand through his hair, his face tense, his eyes bleak. "God that was tough. I…you're right. I'm a lousy father. She's ill because of me. When she started screaming…" He paused and bit his lower lip. "You two are better off without me."

Stunned, Brooke stared at him. "What's that supposed to mean?"

"I can't do this," he said, his eyes beseeching. "I'm not good for her."

"You're giving up? You're deserting us?"

"No, I'm not deserting you. You're better off without me."

"Olivia has a bad cold that she probably caught from the day care center. I felt guilty for being so hard on you. You're giving up?" Brooke threw up her hands, everything she'd feared about Colin suddenly slamming into her. "I was going to apologize for taking this out on you, but I didn't expect you to run. You just needed an excuse."

"No, but you're right. I should never have taken her out in the snow." He ran his hand through his hair again. "Now, I'm leaving…and I'm not going to be here. Having a long-distance relationship is going to be difficult. You guys were better off without me."

Brooke shook her head, unable to comprehend that things had changed so quickly. "So you're just going to give up the first time she gets sick?" she asked in disbelief.

"It's for the best. I don't want to harm her."

"When you were a little boy, was it for the best when your mother left? How do you think Olivia's going to feel?" she asked, reminding herself to keep her voice down when all she wanted to do was scream.

"Damn, Brooke, that's not fair."

"The hell it isn't. At the first illness, you run. What would you have done all the other times she was sick? Kids get sick."

"Remember, I'm the one who didn't want children!"

Anger surged through her, and all the reasons she'd never told him about her pregnancy suddenly seemed to be staring her in the face. "Get the hell out. You're such a coward. You don't deserve to be her father. I thought we had something special but obviously not if you run at the first sign of trouble."

She grabbed her purse and pulled out the jeweler's box, shoving it into his hand. "Keep the freaking ring. You've already broken the promise."

Brooke watched as Colin opened his mouth to speak, and then he turned and walked out the door, closing it softly behind him.

Damn him! When she needed him, he'd realized that parenting wasn't easy. He'd turned chicken and run in the opposite direction.

She sank down on the couch, staring at the Christmas tree with the twinkling lights. Damn him! He'd come back into her life just long enough to make her fall in love with him all over again. And just like before, he'd hurt her.

Tears started to roll down her face, and she couldn't stop the sobs. Once again, she'd fallen for him and he'd broken her heart.

Brooke glanced at the clock. Twelve thirty. Christmas Eve. She'd wait and tell Olivia after Christmas that her father was gone. But not now. Not until she was feeling better and Christmas had passed. She didn't want her daughter's memories of Christmas tarnished with the knowledge that was the day her father had left.

Yet Brooke would always know that Colin had run on Christmas Eve…just like his mother.

~

The next day, Colin sat in the airport terminal waiting for his flight. He glanced at his watch—an hour until takeoff. The speaker overhead announced gate changes to the crowded waiting area, and across the hall they were boarding a plane to Chicago.

His bags were packed. His mail was being forwarded, and he'd arranged for the moving company to pick up his belongings. But this didn't feel like the joyous occasion he'd planned. He didn't feel excited or thrilled at leaving.

For one thing, he hadn't gotten much sleep last night. After leaving Brooke, he'd lain awake all night remembering what she'd said. She'd called him a coward. Was he running from being a father?

He loved Olivia, but he didn't want to damage her the way his mother scarred him. He wanted his daughter to have a safe, normal childhood. Obviously, she wasn't safe with him. He'd taken her out in the snow and made her ill. What other harm would his leaving cause her?

Olivia was a sweet, beautiful child that would be better off without her father around to cause her injury. But hadn't the absence of his mother damaged him? Didn't he still wonder where she was and why she'd left him?

They assumed she was dead, but a small part of him would always wonder why she'd never returned. Had it been voluntary?

His grandmother kept assuring him that his mother would have returned for him if at all possible, but still the little boy inside him missed his mom. And she'd left him on Christmas Eve. Just like he was leaving Brooke and Olivia on Christmas Eve.

He frowned. History was repeating itself. He was leaving, and while he intended to see Olivia again, he didn't want her to remember he'd left on Christmas Eve.

His job required he leave today. He had to be in California, working and running his branch, no later than December 26.

He sat staring out the window at the airplane that was destined to take him to California. This was everything he'd worked hard to achieve.

Brooke's face swam before his eyes, and his chest ached. God, he didn't want to leave her. Yet he'd hurt her when he'd run last night. She'd ended the relationship. Told him to get the hell out and called him a coward.

What was the job compared to the happiness he'd experienced with her and Olivia these last few weeks? The job was just an accomplishment. Brooke had shown him there was so much more to life. With his girls he'd found happiness and a sense of family he'd never experienced before.

And with Brooke he'd found the love that had been missing from his life. He loved her. She made him feel like a strong man capable of tackling the world as long as she was by his side. He needed her. Without her, he was nothing but a salesman, and he wanted so much more.

Being with Brooke and Olivia left him longing for the family he'd never had. He wanted to be a loving husband and was determined to become a good father.

How could he do that while he worked in sunny California? How could he expect Brooke to believe that she was his life, his soul, his very reason for existence? And last night, like the coward she'd called him, he'd been unable to express his feelings for her. He'd never told her he loved her.

This was wrong. This promotion was wrong. This trip was wrong. Everything he'd done in the last twenty-four hours was wrong. Actually, since he'd accepted the position of western sales director, everything had been wrong.

He pulled out his cell phone and dialed the number. "Merry Christmas, Logan."

"Did you call to gloat?" Logan asked.

"No, I called to tell you before I called Ed. Congratulations man, you're the new western sales director."

"What?" Logan said, his voice stunned.

"I don't want to move to California. So I'm passing on the promotion. It's all yours," Colin said.

"Wow! I'm shocked," Logan replied. "Are you sure? Somehow I feel like I'm being punked."

"I'm positive. The position is yours," Colin said. "It's probably impossible for you to catch a plane tonight, but tomorrow they're going to want you on your way to beautiful, warm California. So you better start packing."

"Thanks, man. I appreciate the call. Merry Christmas, and I hope you're happy here."

"Thanks, Logan."

Colin ended the call and then dialed his boss.

"Merry Christmas, Ed. I have to tell you, I'm not taking this position. I've already called Logan and told him it's his."

"What?"

"I understand if you decide to fire me, but it's just not right for me. I need to stay in town with my daughter," Colin said, certain he'd made the right decision. He gave Ed the condensed version of the last month and his daughter.

"Fire my best salesman? Are you kidding me? I understand about family issues. I hope that you can work everything out. In the meantime, I'll see you in the office the day after Christmas." He paused for a moment. "Merry Christmas, Colin."

"Merry Christmas, Ed, I hope it's going to be the best one ever." Colin disconnected the call and glanced at his watch. He had very little time left to get everything he needed.

He hurried out of the airport, determined to win Brooke back.

~

Olivia's fever had broken early that morning, but Brooke kept her in bed all day. The child had complained, but she'd felt bad enough that it hadn't seemed like too much of an imposition. She'd spent the day watching movies and coloring.

Tonight she'd fallen straight asleep. Now Brooke sat putting Christmas toys together and watching the ten o'clock news.

"Breaking news," the television newscaster said. "A Boeing 747 carrying over two hundred passengers bound for Los Angeles has crashed on takeoff at Denver International Airport. It's not known if there are any survivors."

Brooke stopped breathing. She stared at the television. A plane crash. The television showed pictures from the scene of a wrecked plane with smoke spiraling up into the sky as rescue personnel tried to get close to the wreckage.

No, this couldn't be happening. No, Colin was on a plane bound for Los Angeles. No, no, no not Colin.

Brooke's heart leaped into her throat. She felt nauseous and wanted to throw up.

The front of the plane was black from the fire that had consumed at least first class. The back of the plane had broken off, and empty seats were visible to the night sky.

The television voice wouldn't stop. "First responders are saying that it's unknown how many are dead, but that most of the deaths occurred in the first class section."

If that was Colin's plane, his seat was located in first class, and he was on a flight bound to Los Angeles. She grabbed the phone and dialed his cell number. Her pride no longer mattered. It automatically went to voice mail. "Call me as soon as you get this message."

He couldn't be dead. No, not Colin.

In the background, she dimly heard the reporter. "At this time, the injured are being transported to area hospitals. The next of kin will be notified as soon as the bodies are identified. Again, if you're just joining us-Flight 1225 bound for Los Angeles has crashed on takeoff."

Tears streamed down Brooke's cheeks. It was his flight number, and she didn't think anyone in first class could have survived that fire. Colin was dead. She sank to the floor. Great gulping sobs rocked her.

No, this couldn't be happening. He couldn't be dead. She needed him. Sobs rolled through her. She cried for the lost chance they had as a couple. She cried until her eyes were red and swollen and she couldn't breathe.

Exhausted, she went to her closet and pulled out his old college jersey, hugging it to her. She needed Colin, and now he was gone.

She'd planned on giving the shirt back to him but just never gotten the chance. Now she never would.

~

Colin stood outside Brooke's apartment in the Santa suit he'd managed to wrangle from Amelia. Snow started to fall, crystal-like in appearance as it shimmered from the sky. He hoped it added ambiance to his plans, and he prayed for Brooke's forgiveness. He wanted this-them-more than he'd ever wanted the promotion. More than he wanted anything.

He rang the doorbell. Several hours had passed since he'd left the airport to arrange everything. He hoped Brooke was still awake.

The sound of the door lock turned, and then she stood there, her eyes red and swollen from crying.

"What's wrong?" he asked, fear streaking through him like a naked runner. "Is Olivia all right?"

She threw her arms around him. "Oh my God, it's you! You weren't on that plane. You're alive!"

She burst into tears, sobbing against his shoulder, her arms wound tight against his neck, squeezing him like she couldn't get close enough.

"What?" he asked. "You're ruining my setup here."

"Don't you know?" she asked, her voice muffled against his shirt, her arms still around him.

The puppy stuck his head out of the sack and barked.

"I know that I love you so much that I couldn't get on that plane and leave you. I know that in the last four weeks you've changed my life. I'm not a good father, but I promise to try to become a better one if you'll help me. I acted like a fool last night. I'm sorry."

Brooke sobbed against his shoulder even more. Finally, she managed to get her tears under control. "Your plane. It crashed on takeoff. It appears that no one in first class survived."

Shock streaked through Colin, leaving him numb. He would have died if he'd gotten on that plane. The people sitting in the waiting room with him at the airport, some of them were dead. Families and children on that flight, heading home for Christmas, were gone. And he'd lived. He'd be dead right now if he'd chosen not to stay with Brooke and Olivia. Just like his mother had disappeared on Christmas Eve.

Nausea rolled through him at the realization.

"Oh God," he said, pulling Brooke tightly in his arms. "I couldn't leave. I couldn't leave you and Olivia behind. I called Logan and told him the job was his."

He hung onto her, realizing how close he'd come to dying. He'd known for hours now that he'd made the right decision, but to think if he'd chosen wrong he would be dead was frightening. The job wasn't worth dying over.

"I'm so glad you're alive. And I'm glad you gave up the promotion, though I know it meant a lot to you. You're safe, and you're here with me," Brooke said, not releasing him, but hanging on like she never wanted to let go.

Stunned, his mind replayed the same thought. If he'd stayed on the plane, he'd be dead. A soothing calmness overcame him. He'd made the right decision. He'd chosen his girls over money and advancement. And by doing so, he'd chosen life.

He pushed Brooke out of his arms, reached into his bag more determined than ever. He pulled out the jeweler's box. He'd seen the disappointment on her face at dinner and realized he was an idiot.

She didn't want a mother's ring. She wanted an engagement ring with the promise of a future for the two of them. She wanted hearts and flowers and love, and she deserved them.

Colin went down on one knee, determined to get it right this time. He opened the box. She gasped.

"Brooke, I fell in love with you in college, but I was a young shmuck who didn't know how to handle my feelings for you. Will you please give me a second chance to show you how much I love you? Will you be my wife?"

Brooke launched herself into his arms. "Yes. Yes, I love you so much. I always have."

They toppled into the snow. Colin had to catch himself so that he didn't land on the sack of gifts. The puppy leaped out of the bag, happy to be loose. He scampered over to lick Brooke on the chin.

Brooke giggled as she grabbed the animal. "A dog? You bought our daughter a dog after I said no?"

"You said 'our daughter'." He kissed her on the cheek. "That has such a nice sound. Thank you."

Brooke snuggled against him in the snow. "Really, a dog?"

"Well, I was thinking that if you agreed to marry me, we would need a bigger place. A house with a yard. That had been your concern about a dog, right? Is it okay? If not, I'll take him back."

She kissed Colin on the lips, a sweet lingering kiss that promised so much more, before she released him. "Let's go wake up Olivia and tell her Santa arrived early."

The dog barked, sat down in the snow, and wagged its tail at the two of them.

"I think he's anxious to meet his new owner," Colin said.

"Thank you, Colin," Brooke said.

"For what?" he asked.

"For loving me and our daughter. She's going to be thrilled to have a daddy and a dog. I'm so happy you came home, back to me."

"I'm the one who has the best gift this Christmas. I have you and our daughter. I wore this Santa suit because if you hadn't challenged me, I wouldn't have learned that family is more important than money. I would be dead," he said.

Brooke kissed him. "I love you."

"I love you, more," he said. "But where did you get that shirt? It looks like my old jersey from college."

She wiggled her brows at him. "It is, and if you come in, I'll let you take it off."

"You don't have to ask me twice," he said.

The puppy began to chase its tail, barking happily as they stood. When they opened the door, the puppy dashed into the house and ran straight into Olivia's bedroom.

Before they could get to her, she yelled.

"Mom! Santa brought me a puppy!"

Colin looked at Brooke and they smiled. The Christmas memories from his past melted away, and he knew this Christmas would be the memory he held next to his heart.

~

Gabriella shimmered into view and looked down at the happy family. Olivia held the puppy in her arms, and he was licking her face. Colin had his arms around Brooke, and she gazed at him like she would never let him go after coming so close to losing him.

Gabriella knew tonight she would not be singing with the other angels at the celebration of the savior's birth. There was a plane crash to clean up and people to comfort.

"Devon, you're evil!" she yelled into the atmosphere.

A laugh came from the darkness. "You saved Colin's soul. What more do you want?"

"Really? There's going to be a lot of broken hearts tonight thanks to you."

"Deal with it," he said, never appearing before her.

"It's Christmas Eve. Couldn't you at least have had some consideration for the families? A plane crash is a horrible way to make your soul count," Gabriella said, knowing that these were her final minutes with Brooke and Collin and little Olivia. Knowing the success of this case and their love would encourage her in the coming hours and remind her of the good she'd achieved.

"I had to make quota."

"And tomorrow it begins all over again. People are more important than quota! You're a sore loser," Gabriella said.

"Who said I lost?" Devon said. "You'll spend Christmas comforting the victims' families while I'll be celebrating staying out of the pit."

He laughed, the sound pure evil.

Gabriella had heard enough, and she called upon all her strength.

"Evil, be gone," Gabriella said in a booming voice.

"Until next time," Devlin said, flashing briefly before Gabriella and then disappearing.

"Merry Christmas," she said, watching the family below her. Her work here was done. Colin McDermott was a changed man who had found the love he deserved. "Your mother loves you and wishes you a Merry Christmas."

The End!

Thank You For Reading!

Dear Reader,

I hope you enjoyed *The Reluctant Santa* as much as I loved writing this story

I have one small request. If you're inclined, please leave a review. Whether or not you loved the book or hated it, I'd enjoy your feedback.

If you'd like to learn about my new releases as soon as possible, please sign up for my newsletter at: : http://www.sylviamcdaniel.com/newsletter/

Reading one of my books is like spending time with me, and I just want to say thank you from the bottom of my heart.

Sincerely,
Sylvia McDaniel

Books by Sylvia McDaniel

Contemporary Romance

<u>*Standalones*</u>
The Reluctant Santa
My Sister's Boyfriend
The Wanted Bride
The Relationship Coach
Her Christmas Lie
Secrets, Lies, and Online Dating
Paying for the Past
Cupid's Revenge

<u>*Anthologies*</u>
Kisses, Laughter & Love
Christmas with you

Collaborative Series

<u>*Magic, New Mexico*</u>
Touch of Decadence

Western Historicals

<u>*Standalones*</u>
A Hero's Heart
A Scarlet Bride
Second Chance Cowboy

<u>*The Cuvier Women*</u>
Wronged
Betrayed
Beguiled

<u>*Lipstick and Lead*</u>
Desperate
Deadly
Dangerous
Daring
Determined
Deceived

<u>*Scandalous Suffragettes*</u>
Abigail
Bella
Callie
Faith

<u>*The Burnett Brides*</u>
The Rancher Takes a Bride
The Outlaw Takes a Bride
The Marshal Takes a Bride
The Christmas Bride

<u>*Anthologies*</u>
Wild Western Women
Courting the West
Wild Western Women Ride Again

Collaborative Series

<u>*The Surprise Brides*</u>
Ethan

<u>*American Mail Order Brides*</u>
Katie

About the Author

   Sylvia McDaniel is a best-selling, award-winning author of historical romance and contemporary romance novels. Known for her sweet, funny, family-oriented romances, Sylvia is the author of The Burnett Brides, a western historical western series, The Cuvier Widows, a Louisiana historical series, and several short contemporary romances.

   She is the former President of the Dallas Area Romance Authors, a member of the Romance Writers of America®, and a member of Novelists Inc. Her novel, A Hero's Heart, was a 1996 Golden Heart Finalist. Several other books have placed or won in the San Antonio Romance Authors Contest and the LERA Contest, and she was a Golden Network Finalist.

   Married for nearly twenty years to her best friend, they

have two dachshunds that are beyond spoiled and a good-looking, grown son who thinks there's no place like home. She loves gardening, shopping, knitting, and football (Cowboys and Bronco's fan), but not necessarily in that order.

Look for her the first Tuesday of every month at the Plotting Princesses blogspot, and be sure to sign up for her newsletter to learn about new releases and contests. Every month a new subscriber is entered into a drawing for a free book!

She can be found online at: www.sylviamcdaniel.com or on Facebook. You can write to Sylvia at P.O. Box 2542, Coppell, TX 75019.

Looking for a new book to read?

One lie changes the course of three lives...

When Marianne Larson uncovers a truth about her marriage, she sets out to change the course of her life, finding herself along the way. But that journey doesn't come easy as her mother and daughter decide to take a ride of their own–a ride that just might change all of their lives.

While discovering secrets, lies, and the truth about men & dating, three generations and three very different personalities recreate their lives and strengthen their female bond. But what they find might just be what they knew all along…

Sneak Peek into Secrets, Lies, and Online Dating

Marianne Larson stood before the apartment door of her husband's latest fling with his two suitcases in hand, determined, scared, and mad as hell. Birds twittered happy songs in the early spring afternoon in North Dallas, but it could have been a death dirge for all she cared.

Like an overcooked steak, she felt fried, burnt to a crisp —she was emotionally done. She had finally let go of the idea that marriage is forever. Each breath she took felt like a fifty-pound bowling ball resting on her chest.

Marianne dropped the two bulging suitcases onto the concrete walk and waited for the constable to step out of sight. She shoved her blonde hair away from her face, yanked back her shoulders, and lifted her shaking fingers to the doorbell.

Her new life was about to begin.

A shadow filled the peephole, and hushed, panicked voices echoed from inside the apartment. She recognized her adulterous, soon-to-be ex-husband's voice. The door opened as far as the security chain allowed.

A blonde woman peeked through the gap with a too-wide, fake smile. Marianne blinked in disbelief at the girl's thigh high boots, clinging thong, and bustier. A leather whip was still in her hand, the perfect accessory to her dominatrix outfit.

"Marianne! What a surprise."

For a moment, Marianne stared, stunned, before hysterical laughter bubbled up from deep within her. She recognized the girl from the company picnic, but leather? Whips?

At her laughter, the girl's russet eyes darkened.

"Yes, a surprise for both of us. I never knew Daniel was into…" Marianne stumbled over the word "…games." She gathered her wits. "I brought Daniel his clothes."

The woman's dark eyes widened. "Here? Whatever for?"

"Look, I know Daniel is inside. His BMW is in the parking lot. You're not the first one to climb on top of him while earning a promotion, though I see you have a unique way of securing your advancement."

Daniel's reddened face appeared in the doorway, his body hidden by his dominatrix. "Marianne, what are you doing here?"

"Bringing you your clothes."

Marianne gazed upon her college sweetheart, her heart void of the love it once held. Daniel shoved his lover aside, slid back the security chain, and yanked the door open.

"Honey, you know this means nothing."

The view of her husband with a leather choke collar around his neck and a leather thong clinging to his loins brought uncontrollable laughter spewing from her like a fountain. How could she not have known that he was into sexual games?

The constable standing to the side muffled his snicker.

"You're right. Your cheating means nothing anymore." Daniel flinched.

She handed the bulging suitcases to the man she'd once loved.

"Here are your things," Marianne said, trembling from nerves, though she'd never felt more certain in her life. "And Constable Warren has something for you."

The constable stepped into the breezeway. "Are you Daniel Larson?"

"Yes?"

The officer shoved the paperwork into Daniel's hand. "Consider yourself served."

"Marianne?" Daniel questioned, his voice rising as he tore open the envelope. "What the hell is this?"

"It's called a divorce. You've cheated on me for the last

time.”

His dark eyes widened as he scanned the contents of the document.

Daniel lifted his shocked gaze to her. “You can't be serious! You locked me out of our home?”

“Yes. I'll see you in court,” she said, wanting to escape before the scene turned ugly.

His tone became cajoling. “Marianne, honey, we've been married a long time. Because of me, you live a comfortable life. You *need* me to take care of you.”

God, no wonder Daniel was top salesman year after year. “You know, that line worked the first hundred times you used it, but not any longer. I'm done, Daniel.”

Marianne walked off, certain they'd said everything.

Daniel followed her, barefoot, his dog chain clinking on the ground. At noon, most people were at work, but a few stopped to stare.

“Don't do this, Marianne. Think of our daughter.”

She kept marching, each determined step finishing what she should have ended years ago.

“I'll end the affair. I'll change,” Daniel promised.

Marianne whirled around to face him. “Why?”

He stopped, his chain rattling, his expression perplexed by her question. “Because – because you want me to.”

“Do I?” She paused, considering his remark for a few seconds. “And that would last until the next pretty blonde in your office offered you a little booty, and then you'd cheat again.”

Daniel stood half-naked in the open parking lot, a baffled expression on his handsome face. He didn't seem to know how to react.

“Don't do this,” Daniel begged. “I won't give you a divorce.”

“Fine. I wanted to make this quick and to protect our daughter from knowing the truth about her father, but we can do this the hard way. A long, drawn-out legal trial will force me to parade your extra-marital affairs through the courtroom. In the end, I'll be entitled to sixty percent of our assets instead of the normal fifty. And our daughter will know what a douche bag her father is."

His dark eyes burned her. "You wouldn't dare."

"And this little escapade will make for interesting viewing in the courtroom. Wave at the camera, darling."

The detective she'd hired moved from behind the van and waved at him, the red light of the video camera beamed as it recorded his stunned expression. Part of her felt despicable for being so brutal, but the rational part knew he deserved this and more. This time he would not brainwash her into believing she had no choice but to stay.

"You planned this," he said in awe.

"Yes, I did," she admitted, proud that she had pushed aside her fears and done what should have happened years ago.

Daniel gave her a pleading look that reached inside, igniting all the fear locked away. Never again would she return to being the same wife who had tolerated his cheating for at least three years.

"Marianne," his voice changed to the sweet seductive tone that normally convinced her to see things his way. "We've been married a long time, baby. You don't play these kinds of games with me. We have a good life together. We have a daughter."

"I want out."

"You've spent the last eighteen years a stay-at-home mom. Are you going to get a job?" He tried to take her hand, but she stepped out of his reach. "Who's going to hire an older woman with no skills?"